HIPPO IN A HOLE

'This must have happened last night in the storm,' Sipho said. 'The tree probably fell and trapped the baby hippo, or the rain could have made the riverbank very slippery and he slid down and got wedged in the mud.'

'That's why the big hippo won't move,' Levina added. 'It's his mother.'

'We've got to get him out!' Mandy said urgently. 'He could die out of water, couldn't he?'

'We have to face the fact that he may have died already,' Levina told Mandy gently. 'He doesn't seem to be moving at all.'

'Perhaps he's just stuck,' James offered. 'Maybe he's given up struggling.'

'The fact is,' Levina said, 'if he *is* alive, he needs his mother's milk to survive.'

Mandy's mind was racing. Why weren't they doing something? Why were they just sitting here talking? Every part of her wanted to be out of the Jeep and pulling Harry free and reuniting him with his mother.

Animal Ark series

LUCY DANIELS

Hippo
— in a —
Hole

Illustrations by Ann Baum

Hodder
Children's
Books

a division of Hodder Headline

Special thanks to Tanis Jordan
Thanks also to C. J. Hall, B.Vet.Med., M.R.C.V.S., for reviewing
the veterinary information contained in this book.

Animal Ark is a trademark of Working Partners Limited
Text copyright © 2000 Working Partners Limited
Created by Working Partners Limited, London W6 OQT
Original series created by Ben M. Baglio
Illustrations copyright © 2000 Ann Baum

First published in Great Britain in 2000
by Hodder Children's Books

A Catalogue record for this book is available from the British Library

ISBN 0 340 77846 6

Typeset by Avon Dataset Ltd, Bidford-on-Avon, Warks

Printed and bound in Great Britain by
Clays Ltd, St Ives plc

Hodder Children's Books
a division of Hodder Headline
338 Euston Road
London NW1 3BH

One

'Don't forget to bring something warm to wear, Mandy!' Levina Lemiso called over her shoulder, as she started the engine of the Jeep. 'It can be pretty cold when you're out at night, even in South Africa!'

On her way back to the research station where she was working, Levina had called in at the Ubungane Lodge resort where Mandy Hope, her parents and her best friend James Hunter were spending the Easter holidays. The Tanzanian vet had come to invite them on a night safari.

Twelve-year-old Mandy felt a familiar shiver of anticipation at the thought of being out in the African bush after sunset. Right now it was hard to imagine being cold. The hot sun blazed down as she and James dived into the swimming-pool and raced each other to the deep end and back.

'Ten minutes more, you two,' Emily Hope called, getting up from her sun-lounger under a shady palm tree and picking up her book. 'We need to have an early dinner if we're going out this evening.'

'This is the life,' Adam Hope said with a sigh, looking up from his paper. 'One of the guests who arrived from England this morning gave me this. It says it was pouring with rain in Yorkshire yesterday!'

'That won't have pleased Jean,' Mandy said, hauling herself out of the water. 'She hates it when the floor gets all muddy.'

Jean Knox was the receptionist at Animal Ark, the Hopes' busy veterinary practice in Welford, a small village in Yorkshire. Having been rushed off their feet since Christmas, the Hopes had been delighted when Levina, their old friend from veterinary school, had telephoned to say she had a great new job in South Africa and suggested they come out for a holiday.

In a flurry of excitement, flights had been arranged, cover for the practice organised and bags packed. And now it was already the last week of their three-week holiday. Mandy couldn't believe how quickly it had gone. They'd seen masses of wildlife, helped to retrieve some kidnapped leopard cubs that had been separated from their mother, and had even been involved in saving an injured giraffe.

If that wasn't enough action for one holiday, the previous week James had given them all a scare when he'd been bitten on his ankle by a snake. Luckily it had turned out to be non-venomous and James had fully recovered after a couple of days of using a walking-stick.

After their swim, Mandy and James had a quick rinse under the freshwater shower, then gathered up their towels and walked back to their cabin with Mr Hope.

All the cabins were designed in the traditional round style with thatched roofs and cool stone floors, and each one was named after an animal. Adam and Emily Hope were in Eland Lodge which had a carving of an antelope on the door. Mandy and James were next door in Leela's Lodge, which had been named after an orphaned leopard cub who had been hand-reared on-site before being released back into the wild. Mandy was still impressed every time she opened their cabin door and saw all the photographs round the room, tracking Leela's progress.

Mandy quickly changed into long trousers and a shirt and put a sweatshirt in her bag. She took her binoculars from the hook behind the door and went outside to wait for James.

'What do you think we'll see tonight?' Mandy asked, when she and James met up with her parents coming out of Eland Lodge.

'I know Levina is keen to check on a group of hippos,' Mrs Hope said, closing the door. 'Have you both got everything you need?'

'Yep,' Mandy answered, looking at James who nodded.

'Good, then we won't need to come back here,' she said, locking the door.

'Apparently, as there's been so little rain recently a lot of animals have come down to the dam and the lake behind it where there's more water,' Adam Hope explained, as they walked across to the restaurant. 'But there's a group of hippos that are still upstream.'

'They're your favourite animals, aren't they, Dad? I wonder why . . .' Mandy said, with a cheeky grin.

'Because, Mandy,' Mr Hope laughed, 'hippos have the right idea – sleeping and keeping cool in the water most of the day and eating nearly all night. *And* they don't have to watch their weight!'

'I can't imagine a skinny hippo,' James said, grinning.

'I don't think they have such an easy life,' Mandy said. 'Levina told me that the males have terrible fights defending their territory, and sometimes they get badly wounded or killed.'

'That's right,' Emily Hope added. 'And the females have to protect their babies.' She linked arms with her husband. 'You're much better off as a vet.'

As they approached the restaurant, one of

the workers turned on the lanterns that hung in the trees, lighting up the outdoor seating area. 'Let's sit outside,' Adam Hope suggested.

They chose a table and ordered their meal. When their food arrived, they ate it watching a troop of vervet monkeys settling down for the night in a tree nearby. 'I wonder which one of you pinched my scrunchie?' Mandy called up to them, laughing.

The monkeys were used to people and often finished up any leftover food they could find. They also had a habit of sneaking into the cabins and pilfering whatever took their fancy. The Hopes and James had learned the hard way not to leave anything lying around.

'Never mind your scrunchie, Mandy,' her mum said ruefully, 'what about my beads?'

'Since we found out it was them,' James said between mouthfuls, 'I've been watching those monkeys. You know, they go to a waterhole near the acacia trees early every afternoon. Why don't they go at dawn or dusk, like most of the other animals?'

'Because they're very clever, James,' Mr Hope answered. 'They know that just after noon, when it's really hot, is the time when most of the big cats take a siesta. And as animals are very vulnerable to attack when they're drinking, the monkeys realise it's much safer if they wait until their predators are asleep.'

'Hmm, that makes sense,' James agreed, taking a piece of bread from the bowl Mrs Hope was offering him.

After they had finished eating they walked over to the main building to meet Levina. The sun was beginning to set, permeating the sky with hues of pink and red.

When they arrived in reception, the office door opened and Mmatsatsi Ngomane came out carrying a sheaf of papers. 'Hello,' she said, smiling broadly. Mmatsatsi always wore traditional dress and today she had on a blue robe patterned with large golden locusts. 'I hear you're going out with Levina tonight,' she said. 'Have a good time,' She looked at her watch. 'Nearly seven, I must hurry. I need to take these papers over to the dining-room. It's tomorrow's itinerary for the new group of visitors. Look, here comes Levina now.'

A white, open-topped, four-wheel drive Jeep

drove into the compound and pulled up in front of reception. Levina leaned out and called across to them. '*Sawubona*, Mmatsatsi. You're working late!'

Mandy had already learned that *sawubona* was the isiZulu word for hello.

'Isn't Sipho going with you?' Mmatsatsi asked, as she set off to deliver the itineraries. Mmatsatsi's husband Sipho was the manager of the research centre.

'Too busy,' Levina called after her. 'Jump in,' she said, turning to the Hopes and James.

The big, spacious Jeep had seats for eight people. Adam Hope sat beside Levina in the front and Emily Hope sat behind them. Mandy and James each grabbed a back seat. On the front of the Jeep, fixed firmly to the bumper, was a metal seat suspended over the bonnet – with a loop of metal to hold on to. Levina had told them this was called the tracker's seat. Mandy and James had both had a go at sitting there and afterwards had admitted to each other that although it had been exciting it was also a bit scary when the Jeep accelerated and they were bumped up and down.

'Right, we'll go straight to the wallow to look for the hippos,' Levina said. She swung the Jeep on to the road. 'The rangers who took a party out today said there was a herd just above the dam in a wallow on a side river. They come out to feed after sunset, so we should get there in time to watch them graze for a while.'

'They eat grass, don't they?' Mandy asked Levina.

'That's right, Mandy, mostly grass,' Levina said. 'Though sometimes they'll nibble shrubs.'

'Do they eat together, like cows in a field?' James asked.

'Good question, James,' Levina said. 'You would expect them to, wouldn't you? But although hippos can be very friendly and sociable with each other in the water, the minute they come out on to land they become solitary animals. Strange, isn't it?'

'Do you think that has something to do with the fact that they don't stay in the same herd for long?' Emily Hope asked, 'I mean, elephants stay in the same herd for years and years.'

'Probably,' Levina said. 'In a hippo herd there's usually a bull and his females but others come and go.' She slowed the Jeep. 'Just look at that sunset!'

The sun had turned a rich orange and was now almost below the horizon. All around, the sky was ablaze with red, yellow and black streaked clouds.

'Dawn and sunset are my favourite times in Africa,' Adam Hope announced. 'Absolutely spectacular.'

As the sun disappeared and the sky darkened, Levina turned on to a dirt track and picked up speed. Mandy looked back at the dam and the vast lake behind it. During the day she loved to watch the different animals that came to drink and swim in the water. Just this morning she had woken James when a big martial eagle circled over the lake before flying off to the rocks to hunt hyraxes. Now the still water looked cold and black in the gloom. She nudged James and pointed at the lake. James turned and looked.

'It looks a bit spooky in the dark, doesn't it?' Mandy said.

'Makes you wonder what might be in there,' James agreed.

As they watched, a full moon emerged from

behind a cloud and lit the lake with a silvery glimmer. 'A full moon for us tonight,' Levina said. 'That's good. In the old days, they called it a hunter's moon because it gave the men more light.'

She drove across a plain where tall bushes and shrubs had been heavily grazed by elephant and giraffe. They were following a wide river that meandered slowly down to feed the lake.

'The river is looking very low,' Levina said anxiously. 'If we don't get more summer rain there will be a drought. The grass won't grow and there won't be enough food or water for all the animals.'

Levina steered away from the main river and drove across a vast open stretch of grassy shrubland dotted with huge baobab trees, before pulling up under some acacias. She manoeuvred the Jeep until its headlights were shining on a strip of water. 'Apparently this is where they saw the hippos today,' Levina told the others, raising her binoculars. 'I wonder if they're still here or if they've left to graze.'

About thirty metres away, a stream that led to the main river had formed a large pool.

Mandy looked through her glasses and saw that the pool seemed to be full of boulders. 'How did all those boulders get there, Levina?' she asked, puzzled.

'Have they been washed down from the mountains?' James suggested.

'Just wait, you two,' Levina chuckled. 'All will be revealed.'

'Oh,' Mandy suddenly exclaimed, 'one's moving!'

The pool erupted in a shower of muddy water and a huge hippo stood up, seeming to stare right at them.

'They looked just like smooth rocks!' James said. 'If you didn't know better, you'd want to walk across them!'

'I wouldn't recommend that, James!' Levina said, laughing. 'They might *look* like friendly, lumbering animals but they can be very dangerous. If a hippo charges then you have to try to get out of its way. Dodging is best as they can easily outrun a human. Look,' she continued, 'that's the big male of the herd. Can you see those scars across his neck?'

Mandy and James both lifted their binoculars

to try and focus on the hippo, but he was lumbering up the bank now, swaying from side to side and churning up the mud with his feet.

'Got him!' Mandy announced, steadying her binoculars on the bar between the seats. 'Those scars are huge! They go right from the back of his neck round to his throat.'

'Yep, I can see them too.' James was silent for a moment. 'Gosh, each one is about two centimetres wide!'

'I was upriver a while ago and I watched him defending his territory,' Levina explained. 'It was terrifying. He fought another male for nearly an hour in the river. When I saw his opponent slash this one's neck with his tusks I felt sure he was beaten. But he fought back and saw the other one off.'

'The other hippo must have been severely injured too!' Adam Hope exclaimed.

'He was,' Levina said, nodding. 'I think he'd lost an eye before he backed off and gave up the fight.'

'Sensible chap,' Emily Hope said. 'Knowing when to give up can be life-saving in certain situations.'

Mandy couldn't take her eyes off the hippos as one by one they left the wallow. She gasped with pleasure as a small baby hippo followed its mum out of the pool, slipping in the mud the adults had churned up. 'Oh look,' she murmured, 'isn't it sweet?'

'That calf is about a year old, I should think, Mandy,' Levina explained, 'judging by its size.'

They all watched as the little hippo trundled along after its mother. It just reached the top of her leg.

'Look, Mandy and James!'

Her dad's excited voice had Mandy on the edge of her seat refocusing her binoculars. Nudged by its mother, an even smaller hippo was struggling to get up the bank. Mandy couldn't take her eyes off it. 'It's *tiny*!' she said. 'How old do you think that one is, Levina?'

But before Levina had a chance to answer, the baby hippo lost its footing and slid on its bottom back down the slope. It looked so funny that everybody laughed as they waited to see what would happen. The hippo struggled to get on its feet to reach its mother again. She manoeuvred herself behind it and with her nose

pushed it up the bank. But the little hippo's front feet sank in the mud and it toppled over on to its nose. When it eventually regained its balance, it gave a violent snort that blew the mud out of its nostrils. Meanwhile its mother pushed it further up the bank, finally giving it a hearty shove over the top. Mandy was laughing so much, she could hardly keep her binoculars still.

At last she was able to steady her hands and fix her sight on the baby as its mother sniffed it to check it over. 'Isn't it gorgeous?' she said, mesmerised. 'I think hippos might be *my* favourite animal now too, Dad.'

'I know what you mean,' Levina said swivelling round in her seat. 'He's very appealing isn't he?'

'How old is he?' James asked.

'He's really young,' Levina said, frowning in thought. 'About two months old, I'd guess. A mother won't let any other hippos near its baby for the first two weeks of its life. She won't return to the herd until she has bonded with it.'

Mandy carefully studied the baby animal as she listened to Levina. She could just see it had three fat little toes on the end of each of its short, dumpy legs. Its body looked tubby and healthy. *For such big animals, hippos have very small eyes,* Mandy thought. 'Oh no!' she said with concern. 'Look, he's got a bit missing from one ear.'

'That's probably one of the other male calves getting too rough with him. The males do wrestle with each other in sham fights,' Levina said, picking up her own binoculars to study the ear. 'The trouble is, hippos close their ears when they go under water and if too much of it is missing it could cause him a problem. It looks like it's only the tip though. I'm sure he'll be all right.'

'He's *much* too little to fight,' Mandy said, feeling upset that such a small animal might get pushed around in a herd. 'He could easily get hurt, couldn't he?'

'I think he's probably tougher than he looks,' her mum said gently, 'and don't forget, Mandy, his mother is very protective and will watch over him constantly.'

Mandy nodded. Her mum was always the voice of reason. 'Has he got a name?' she asked Levina.

'No, I haven't named him yet. But you and James can choose a name if you want to, Mandy,' Levina said, turning to watch the little hippo. 'Why not? Let's have a naming ceremony now.'

'Let's call him Horatio,' James suggested.

'Horatio!' Mandy exclaimed, screwing up her nose. 'That's not a hippo sort of name.'

'That's a very honourable name, Mandy,' Adam Hope said. 'Admiral Nelson's name was Horatio. And I knew a boy at school called Horatio; we used to call him Horry.'

Mandy thought quickly. 'Horry,' she said. 'It's not quite right. It sounds a bit old-fashioned. What about Harry? That would suit him while he's a baby *and* when he grows up to be a huge two-ton hippo and the head of a herd.'

'Maybe we can come back one day and see him,' Emily Hope said, shivering in the chill night air and pulling her sweater over her head.

'Do you think we'd be able to find Harry again?' James asked Levina.

'I don't see why not,' Levina said. 'He'll be recognisable by that missing piece of ear. Plus, hippos follow ancient paths, so these hippos will have used this wallow for years and will continue to do so as part of one herd or another.'

'How far will they go tonight?' Adam Hope asked.

'Two, maybe three, kilometres. They might go to another wallow like this or they might go to the lake,' Levina said. She gave a chuckle. 'They certainly won't go as far as Huberta, though.'

'Huberta?' Mandy asked in a puzzled voice. 'Who's Huberta?'

Two

'Huberta was a hippo born a long time ago not far from here in the Natal province,' Levina explained. 'One day she strolled into a town and found it to her liking. So she stayed. She would walk around eating the shrubbery in people's gardens. The locals came to love her and would feed her. Then one day . . .' Levina paused, looking round at her attentive audience, 'Huberta decided to move on and began walking down the coast. She became a great character and soon everyone had heard about Huberta.'

Mandy listened, spellbound. She couldn't help smiling at the thought of a hippo going off travelling. 'Tell us more, Levina. What happened to her?' she asked eagerly.

'Well, one time Huberta fell asleep on the railway line,' Levina said slowly.

'Oh no!' James groaned. 'She didn't get hit, did she?'

'No, an engine driver gently nudged her out of the way with his train,' Levina said with a broad grin. 'Three years and sixteen hundred kilometres later, Huberta arrived at the Keiskamma river on the Cape coast.'

'That's an amazing story, Levina,' Mandy's dad said. 'Sixteen hundred kilometres! I suppose she was quite a celebrity by then.'

'That's right, Adam, everybody in South Africa knew about Huberta by then.' Levina stopped and looked seriously at Mr Hope. 'Everybody except the hunters who shot her. *They* claimed they had never heard of her.'

Mandy gasped at the dramatic turn of the story. 'That's horrible,' she burst out. 'Poor Huberta! I'm glad there's no hunting of hippos any more.'

'There's still poaching, Mandy,' Levina said seriously. 'In some countries hippo are hunted for their meat and ivory. But, as you can see, the hippos are doing very well here.' She smiled. 'Come on, now. Let's follow them while they graze.'

In the light of the full moon Mandy could clearly see the big bull hippo eating the coarse grass. 'Do hippos ever get toothache?' she asked. She knew that other grass-eating animals sometimes did if they chipped or cracked a tooth.

'I'm sure they do, Mandy, but hippos actually use their lips rather than their teeth to pull at the grass,' Levina told her. 'Each one is very tough and about sixty centimetres in width. Hippos are vegetarian – like you – but they eat about forty-five kilos of food every night!'

'Grandad could do with a hippo in Welford,' Emily Hope said, smiling. 'Then he wouldn't have to mow the lawn.' Adam Hope's parents lived in the same village as Mandy and her mum and dad. Tom Hope was a keen gardener.

'It might eat more than the lawn, Mum!' Mandy said, giggling at the thought of her gran finding a hippo in the garden at Lilac Cottage.

Mandy watched Harry's mother as she carefully avoided treading on the little hippo running around her feet. Every so often he'd run under her tummy and out the other side. When he stopped to suckle, Mandy could hear him slurping as he drank his mother's milk. Gradually the hippos moved further and further away.

'Let's start back now,' Levina said, as Harry and his mum went out of sight.

'Why don't you sit in the tracker's seat, Dad?' Mandy suggested innocently, grinning at James.

'Yes – it's really exciting, Mr Hope,' James added.

'Oh, I don't know,' Emily Hope said, turning round and winking at them. 'I think it might be a bit too bumpy for Adam.'

'Too bumpy!' Adam Hope spluttered with indignation. He was already climbing out of the Jeep. 'Are you implying I'm too feeble to put up with a few bumps? I'm made of sturdier stuff than that.'

Once Mr Hope was seated and holding on, Levina urged him to turn on the powerful spotlight. Slowly she drove off.

'Hey, this is great!' Adam Hope enthused, shining the beam from side to side.

When they reached open savannah Levina began to drive faster. Mr Hope, clinging hard to the metal handle on the bonnet, bounced up and down, almost flying out of the seat at one point. Mandy and James could hardly control their laughter.

Ten minutes later Levina pulled up outside reception.

'I feel like I've been on a bucking bronco!' Adam Hope said, gingerly climbing down. 'I suppose I asked for that.' He grinned ruefully.

'Everybody falls for it, Adam,' Levina told him. 'Mandy and James did. I haven't caught you out yet though, Emily, have I?'

'Count me out, Levina,' Mandy's mum laughed. 'I've been on one before. Come on you two, time for bed.'

'I'll be going out again tomorrow if anyone wants to come along.' Levina looked from Mandy to James. 'Any takers?'

'Yes, please! Can we, Mum, Dad?' Mandy begged.

'I don't see why not,' Adam Hope agreed. He ruffled Mandy's hair. 'What about you, James?'

'I'd love to,' James nodded, stifling a yawn. 'As long as I get some sleep first.'

'Good. I'll see you tomorrow then,' Levina said as she pulled away. '*Hamba kahle*, go well.'

'*Sala kahle*, Levina, stay well.' Mandy answered happily. She could hardly wait to go out to the hippo herd and see Harry again.

It was late the next morning, when Mandy woke up. She was usually up at dawn to watch the animals that came to drink and swim in the lake but she had been exhausted when they got back from their night safari and had slept through the early morning noises. She woke up James and they hurriedly put on T-shirts and shorts and went outside. The sun was shining, but the sky was hazy and the air hot and sultry.

Mandy's dad was coming up the path, whistling cheerfully. 'Good morning,' he said. 'I was just coming to get you. You'll miss breakfast if you don't hurry.'

'Come on!' said James, looking worried and setting off at a run.

Mandy caught up with James just outside the restaurant where Emily Hope was finishing her coffee.

'What are your plans for today?' Mandy's mum asked, offering them a big bowl of fruit and some hot crusty rolls.

'David said he's got something he wants to show us,' Mandy said, scooping up the last piece of sweet orange mango flesh in the bowl. David was the McKenzie's thirteen-year-old son and she and James had made friends with him and his younger sister, Sophie, who was nine.

'There's a *braai* tonight in the restaurant,' Mrs Hope reminded them. 'You'll just have time for something to eat before you go out with Levina.'

'Brilliant,' James said, rubbing his hands together. Mandy knew that he loved the African-style barbecues and wouldn't miss one even if it was to go on safari. 'I hope they cook those delicious sausages again!' he continued. 'What were they called?'

'You mean *boerewors*, James; good hearty stuff,' Adam Hope said, coming back to finish his breakfast. 'It means farmer's sausage, apparently.'

'Let's go, James,' Mandy said, draining her glass and standing up. 'How can you think about food when we've only just had breakfast?'

They met up with David at the back of the main building. Sipho and Mmatsatsi's daughter, Lindiwe, was with him. Lindiwe and David were best friends, rather like her and James, Mandy thought.

David had a pitchfork in his hand and Lindiwe carried a bundle of clean straw. Strutting sedately across the compound towards them was Lindiwe's pet ground hornbill, Kubi. He was a huge bird, as big as a turkey, completely black with an enormous beak. His red-ringed eyes had long black eyelashes and his face and throat were covered with bare red skin. When she had first introduced Mandy and James to Kubi, Lindiwe had explained that male hornbills had red skin, while females had blue skin.

Now the hornbill's deep booming call resounded in the still air as he stopped in front of Mandy and demanded she scratch his head.

'Have you seen Jackie Hangman since you've been in Africa?' David called, as they crossed the compound to stroke Ushukela, his eland. The big antelope bent his head and nuzzled at the pocket of Mandy's shorts until she fished out the piece of apple she had brought him.

'Jackie Hangman?' James wrinkled up his nose in surprise. 'Who's he?'

'Follow me,' David said, turning and striding off towards the research centre, Lindiwe close on his heels. They were both thirteen and nearly the same height, but David's tanned skin and straight, sun-bleached hair contrasted with Lindiwe's dark skin and black curls. Mandy and James hurried to keep up, eager to know what their friend was referring to.

When they arrived at the centre, Lindiwe led the way to a series of enclosures where animals were sometimes kept. When Mandy got closer she could see that lines of insects had been carefully impaled on the barbed-wire fence; there were worms and locusts, even a small frog.

'This is Jackie Hangman's larder,' David told them proudly. 'He hangs his catch up to dry.

He's just a little bird – fiscal shrike is his proper name, but here in South Africa we call him Jackie Hangman.'

'It makes him sound very impressive,' James commented. 'More like a big vulture.'

'I hear that we now have a baby hippo called Harry,' said a deep voice behind them.

Mandy turned to see a big man coming out of the centre. It was Sipho Ngomane and he was grinning broadly.

David and Lindiwe looked curiously at Mandy.

'Are you going to name *all* the wild animals here, Mandy?' Lindiwe said, raising her eyebrows.

'No,' Mandy said firmly, 'just Harry. He's special. We saw him last night when we were out with Levina; he's only two months old and he's gorgeous!'

'And he looks like a Harry,' James put in, defending Mandy.

'I think Harry the hippo has a nice ring to it,' Sipho said. He put his hands on his hips and looked up at the sky. 'There's a storm in the air you know. I can smell it.'

'Levina says you desperately need rain,'

Mandy commented.

'That's right, Mandy, we do, but a local storm doesn't bring enough to raise the river levels much,' Sipho told her. 'What we need is heavy rainfall in the mountains. That will fill hundreds of streams and creeks and then all the water will pour straight down into this river and fill up the lake behind the dam.' Sipho grinned at Mandy and James. 'Then there will be a herd of very happy hippos!'

Mandy smiled to herself at the thought of Harry splashing about in the river. She'd secretly hoped that someone from the centre might have been going out today, but everyone seemed busy – it looked as if she'd just have to wait until tonight to visit the hippo herd again.

Just then, as if to prove Sipho right, there was a rumble of distant thunder.

'Don't stray too far away this afternoon,' Sipho called to them, as he walked towards the Jeep. 'You don't want to be caught out in a storm.'

'Shall we stay here and help you clean out Ushukela's shed?' Mandy asked David and Lindiwe, as they walked back. Although she was having a fantastic holiday, she occasionally missed Animal Ark and her daily chores looking after the animals.

'Thanks,' David said. 'I'm scrubbing out the shed today, if you feel like helping.'

'Then we'll just have time for a swim before we have to go and change for the *braai*,' James said happily.

As they worked into the afternoon it grew darker, and by the time they had finished, the air had become very hot and still. They all contributed to scrubbing the floor of Ushukela's shed until it shone, then David lay down clean straw while James filled the antelope's bowl with fresh water.

When they eventually stepped outside, Mandy looked anxiously at the darkening horizon. A stiff breeze was blowing and a solid mass of black cloud was coming towards them, like a heavy blanket being drawn across the sky. 'Uh oh!' she said to James, 'I don't think we'll get that swim. Why don't you come to Leela's Lodge and play cards with us instead?' she said, turning to David and Lindiwe.

They were only halfway across the compound

when there came a cracking, like gunshots being fired from the sky, right above them. A wind so strong that it tore leaves from the trees lifted Mandy's baseball cap from her head, and she had to clamp it down quickly with both hands.

'Head for the main building!' David called urgently, as huge drops of rain burst on the dry red dust.

Within seconds the ground was slippery mud that spattered up their legs. Mandy felt her T-shirt flapping wetly against her body as she ran. She could hardly see where she was running because the fierce rain ran into her eyes. They reached reception and fell inside just as the first flash of lightning lit the camp, followed immediately by a tremendous clap of thunder.

'Thank goodness you're in the dry,' Emily Hope said, sounding relieved. 'We were in here talking to Tony and Pam when it started, and wondered where you were.'

'I don't know about being in the dry,' Adam Hope chuckled. 'They couldn't be wetter if they'd swum in the river!'

Mmatsatsi came into reception with big fluffy

towels and a pile of clean T-shirts for them to change into. 'It looks as if we're all going to be stuck here for a while,' she said, handing them out. 'Where is your father, Lindiwe?'

'I think he's gone to pick Levina up from the dam,' Lindiwe answered.

'I hope they're safe and sheltering somewhere,' her mother said, going behind the desk and turning on the lights. 'It's like night-time outside.'

Mandy watched the storm through the glass doors, fascinated. She knew that tropical storms were usually very violent but brief. The rain was still streaming down, puddling on the wooden tables and benches.

'Wow,' James said, as sheet lightning lit up the scene outside like daylight. 'Look! There's a troop of monkeys in that tree covering their heads with leaves.'

'Monkeys don't like getting wet, James,' Lindiwe said, grinning at him. 'Here comes Daddy,' she called to her mother.

They watched as the Jeep pulled up outside. Its canvas roof had filled up with water. Holding up umbrellas, Levina and Sipho made a dash for cover.

'We waited it out as long as possible and then decided to take a chance,' Levina said, shaking her umbrella outside and taking the towel that Emily offered her. 'This *is* a big storm!'

Tony McKenzie came in from a back room. 'We've just lost the roof off one of the cabins,' he told them all in a worried voice. 'I've been meaning to fix it all week but I've been short-staffed. Two of my rangers have taken a party up-country to walk a wilderness trail and one is in town and won't be back until tomorrow.'

'I'll give you a hand later, when the weather's improved,' Adam Hope offered.

'Thanks, Adam.' Tony flashed him a grin. 'That would be helpful. As I'm sure you know, every so often out here nature lets us know who's boss.'

Pam McKenzie came in with steaming mugs of hot chocolate and passed them around. 'The rangers have just called,' she said, shaking her head. 'They saw the storm was heading this way. It's brilliant sunshine up there so that's good for them, especially as they're camping out.' She sighed. 'Well, I suppose we'd better think about eating something.'

'Oh,' James said, his face falling, 'does that mean there won't be a *braai*?' He blushed as everyone laughed.

'Don't worry, we'll prepare some food inside, James,' Pam said, doing a quick head count.

Suddenly all the lights went out. There was a flash of lightning and Mandy could see everyone's faces illuminated. It reminded her of a horror film.

'Don't worry, I'll fetch some lamps,' Tony said confidently. 'The storm must have knocked the generator out.'

As afternoon turned into evening, it stopped raining but the lightning still flashed. Mandy looked inquiringly over at Levina.

'I'm sorry, Mandy, I know how disappointed you must be,' Levina said gently, obviously reading her thoughts. 'But there's no way we can go out tonight in this storm. We'll try again tomorrow.'

Mandy bit her lip. She was deeply disappointed but she knew Levina was right.

'Never mind, Mandy. Look on the bright side, I bet Harry likes the rain,' James said. 'It might be the first storm he's ever seen.'

Mandy tried to hide her disappointment by concentrating on the action of the storm. Suddenly she screwed up her eyes and peered across at the research centre. 'Sipho, your roof is loose. Look!' she cried. 'Wait until the lightning flashes again.'

Everybody rushed from their seats and peered out through the glass doors. Sipho and Mmatsatsi opened them up to get a better view. Sure enough, with the next flash they saw that a section of the corrugated iron roof of the research centre had come loose and was hanging precariously over the veranda.

'Is our house all right, Daddy?' Lindiwe asked, her face set in a frown.

'Yes. It's the research centre roof,' Sipho replied. 'Anyway, at least it's stopped raining. Perhaps the storm will begin to calm down a little now.' He sounded cautious. 'Let's just hope the roof holds.'

While Pam McKenzie and Mmatsatsi went off to make some sandwiches, Sophie went to fetch her game of Trivial Pursuit. 'The Hopes and James against the McKenzies and the Ngomanes,' Sophie decided when she returned. She was blonde like her brother and every bit as friendly.

'That's not fair, there's only three of us,' Lindiwe grumbled good-naturedly.

'Ah, you're forgetting Levina!' Sipho told her. 'She can be in our team.'

Soon they were munching pancakes stuffed with cheese, slicing up fresh avocados and firing questions at each other in the blue lamplight.

Sipho was proved right, and by the time they'd finished eating and the Hopes had won the game, the storm had passed and the air was fresh again. It was almost midnight when, by torchlight, the Hopes and James made their way back along the dark walkways to their cabins.

'Two late nights in a row,' Emily Hope said, as Mandy pushed open the door of Leela's Lodge. 'You'll be asleep before your heads hit the pillow.' She planted a kiss on Mandy's head and yawned. 'And so will I!'

'Sleep well,' Adam Hope said. He shone the torch for them to find their way inside, then he and Mrs Hope made their way into Eland Lodge.

* * *

Mandy felt as if her head had only just hit the pillow when she heard James moving about. 'James, what are you doing? It's the middle of the night!'

'No, it isn't,' James chuckled. 'It's nearly dawn. I think there's something caught on the roof. The thatch has been rustling nearly all night. Didn't you hear it?'

'No,' Mandy replied. 'I hardly even remember getting into bed. Where are you taking that chair?'

'I'm going to climb up and have a look,' James said, struggling to carry the big wooden armchair outside.

By the time Mandy had thrown on her clothes and dashed after James, he was standing on the chair peering into the thatch.

'There's definitely something here,' he said in a hushed voice, 'but I can't quite see it.' James was standing on tiptoe now, stretching up as far as he could. Suddenly he looked down at Mandy. 'If you hold the chair I can stand on the arms and then I'll be able to have a proper look. It could be an animal.'

'Oh, it might be hurt!' Mandy exclaimed, taking a grip on the legs of the chair.

Holding tightly to the thatch James balanced on the arms and pulled himself up. 'I can see now, it's . . . uh oh . . .' His voice was alarmed.

'What is it, James?' Mandy said desperately. 'Are you all right?'

James looked down at her, his face white. 'Sorry! I thought it was a snake at first! But I think it's a tail,' he said, relief flooding into his voice. 'Somehow whatever it is has found its way under a section of thatch. I'm going to try to coax it down.' From her crouched position, Mandy saw James stretch out an arm and push the thatch away as much as he could. Then he cried out. 'Oh, you poor thing!'

'What is it, James?' Mandy asked. 'Tell me, I can't stand the suspense!'

James's worried face peered down at her again. 'It's a monkey and it's injured. It's holding its arm at a funny angle. I've tried to get it to come to me, but it won't budge.'

Mandy thought quickly. She had an idea. 'Hold tight and don't move, James. Just for one second.'

Balanced on the chair, James hung on to the thatch and kept absolutely still. He obviously sensed that if he moved a leg the chair would tip up.

Mandy dashed into Leela's Lodge, and was back in a flash. Carefully she stood on the seat and passed James a biscuit and a piece of banana. 'See if you can tempt it with these,' she said, getting down and holding the chair steady.

James held the banana out to the monkey and waited. The monkey didn't move.

'What's happening?' Mandy asked.

'I'm holding the banana out for it, but it doesn't seem interested,' James told her. 'And my arm is beginning to ache.'

'Try the biscuit!' Mandy told him.

They'd seen the vervet monkeys that lived in the trees around the resort come down and pinch bits of broken biscuits that the tourists left. They always seemed to be hungry.

'OK,' James agreed. There was a pause and then he spoke up again. 'Wow, it's really showing an interest now. Come on, take a bite,' he urged the monkey. 'That's it!' Without turning his head he told Mandy what was going on. 'It's eaten a piece of biscuit and now I'm trying to tempt it nearer. It's coming. It's nibbling some more biscuit and I can almost get hold of it.'

Mandy could see the monkey nearly at the edge of the thatch.

Bang! A cabin door slammed.

To her horror, Mandy saw the monkey throw itself at James's head and, before she could do anything to help, James lost his balance and toppled backwards, falling with a thud on to the grass.

'James!' she screamed, throwing herself on her knees beside his still body. Mandy's heart froze. James wasn't moving.

Three

'Mandy!' Mrs Hope came flying out of Eland Lodge closely followed by her husband, both of them in pyjamas. 'What on earth's happening? James! Oh my goodness!' Kneeling down beside Mandy, she took James's arm and felt for a pulse.

James groaned.

'It's all right, James,' Mrs Hope reassured him softly. 'He's just winded, Mandy, but it looks like he's hurt his wrist.' She nodded at James's other hand.

'Do you think it's broken?' Mandy asked her mum.

'I won't know until I examine it properly, but I hope not,' Emily Hope said.

James's eyes slowly flickered open. He looked at Mrs Hope and then at Mandy. 'Is the . . . ah . . . monkey all right?' he asked in a breathless voice.

The monkey lay half hidden underneath the fallen armchair, a pathetic heap of fur, with eyes closed and one arm bent the wrong way.

'The monkey is probably winded, just like you, James,' Adam Hope told him. As he spoke, Mr Hope picked up the monkey, put it on the table and gently began examining it.

It was typical of James to worry about the animal before himself, but Mandy was really worried about her friend. 'How do you feel?' she asked him anxiously.

'I . . . can't . . . seem to . . . breathe properly,' James gasped. 'I feel . . .' he gulped in air, 'like my spine . . . collided . . . with my . . . ribs.' He tried a weak smile and winced.

'Now, don't try to move,' Mrs Hope ordered. 'You've had a nasty fall and I'm afraid you've done some damage to your wrist. Mandy, run to reception and tell the McKenzies to radio for a doctor. Quick as you can!'

Mandy didn't need telling twice. With the speed of an Olympic runner she raced to the main building. This was the second time this holiday that she'd gone to get medical help for James! After the storm and the late night the place was all shut up and everybody was still in bed. She ran around the building banging on the window shutters and shouting for help.

An upstairs window opened and Tony McKenzie looked out. 'What on earth is going on down there?' he asked crossly. 'It sounds like a bunch of baboons has hit camp.'

'Mr McKenzie,' Mandy gasped, 'there's been an accident. James fell off the roof of Leela's Lodge!' Suddenly she found she was sobbing and shaking uncontrollably.

Tony McKenzie's head disappeared into the room. Moments later, Mandy heard bolts being drawn back. Mr McKenzie opened the door and came out with his wife, Pam. Both their faces showed their concern. Pam put her arm round Mandy's shoulders and guided her back to the cabin. Tony hurried alongside. Mandy filled them in on what had happened.

'But what was he doing up there in the first place?' Tony McKenzie asked in a bewildered voice.

'He was trying to rescue an injured monkey,' Mandy said earnestly.

The McKenzies exchanged glances and Mandy thought she saw a smile flicker on Tony McKenzie's face.

'I might have guessed it would have something to do with animals,' he said kindly. In the short time the McKenzies had known Mandy and James they had already learned how much they cared about animals.

Back at Leela's Lodge, James was sitting in a chair, his arm wrapped in a thick wet towel. Adam Hope stood beside him, holding the monkey. The McKenzies went straight over to talk to Emily Hope.

Mandy squatted down beside James. 'How are you doing?' she asked in a faint voice, not feeling very well herself.

James managed a weak grin. 'I felt a bit funny when your mum examined my wrist. It hurt quite a lot,' he told her. 'And she thinks I've

sprained it. Oh, Mandy, I won't have to go to hospital, will I?' His voice trembled as he spoke.

Mandy realised they were both probably suffering from shock. 'Mum and Dad will know what's best for you, James,' she said as calmly as she could. 'Trust them.'

Adam Hope was wrapping the monkey in a sweatshirt. 'This little one has a broken wrist, James,' he said with a sigh. 'It appears to have happened a while ago. So when you found it, it must already have been in pain. That was probably why it was reluctant to come out from the thatch at first. It's my bet it was blown out of a tree in the storm and landed on your roof.'

'How did it get *under* the thatch though, Dad?' Mandy asked in a puzzled voice.

'It was probably frightened by the storm,' Adam Hope replied. 'Animals do strange things when they're scared.'

'Adam,' Emily Hope said to her husband. 'We have a small problem. Tony found the radio mast down last night, so it's going to be hard to contact a doctor.'

'What are our alternatives?' Adam Hope asked, rubbing his chin thoughtfully.

'It's feeling better already, Mrs Hope,' James put in optimistically. 'I'm sure it's nothing much.' The colour had come back into his face and he moved the towel to look at his wrist. 'It doesn't hurt too much to move it and it's not swelling any more either.'

'We have a fully equipped first-aid box,' Pam told Emily Hope, 'if you want to strap it up yourself.'

'James, we have to do the best for you,' Mrs Hope told him as she bent over to inspect his wrist. 'We are responsible for you, so please don't make light of any pain.'

'Honestly, Mrs Hope,' James insisted. 'It really *doesn't* hurt so much.'

'Can you wiggle your fingers?' Adam Hope asked, as he too took a look.

'Yep.' James wiggled his fingers to prove it.

'Come along, then,' Emily Hope said, helping James to his feet. 'We'll strap it up to give it some support, but *please* don't use it for a few days. Give the sprain a chance to heal.'

Mandy took the monkey from her father. 'You will set the monkey's arm, Mum, won't you?'

'Of course, Mandy,' Emily Hope replied. 'Bring it along.'

'The little thing's had a crack on the head too,' Adam Hope told them. 'She's got a lump the size of a hazelnut so she's probably a bit concussed.'

Mandy sat in reception holding the monkey while her Mum bandaged James's arm in the first-aid room. Adam Hope had splinted the monkey's arm so she couldn't move it and given her a mild sedative to keep her calm.

Mandy was relieved that James's wrist wasn't broken. 'Poor James,' she whispered softly to the monkey, 'and poor you.' Mandy stroked the monkey's head. Her honey-coloured fur had an almost greenish tinge but her face was a perfect heart shape of black fur.

At that moment the door of the first-aid room opened and Emily Hope came out. 'Here we are,' she said with a big smile.

James followed her out, looking a lot happier. Bandage covered most of his hand and wrist; only his fingers and thumb stuck out. 'It hardly hurt at all,' he told Mandy with a grin.

'James can watch the monkey have her arm set, and then he must have a rest. It's been quite a traumatic morning,' Adam Hope said, coming up behind James and putting his hands on his shoulders. 'Mandy, can you carry the monkey through?'

Mandy stood up carefully with the little creature in her arms. She took the monkey into the first-aid room and then they all watched as Emily Hope worked quickly, deftly setting the arm and winding on a bandage.

'Right,' said Mrs Hope, 'she'll need to be kept quiet, like James, for a while. The sedative will begin to wear off and, as she's a wild animal,'

she said seriously to Mandy and James, 'you'll
have to be careful that she doesn't bite you.'

As Mandy's mum spoke, the monkey's eyes
opened and began to flicker in terror. Though
she was used to people from living on the
compound, she'd probably never been inside a
building before. She whimpered softly as Mandy
scooped her up gently. Then the little monkey
snuggled herself down in the sweatshirt.

'She knows you already, Mandy,' James said.

'Why don't you take her over to the centre
and ask Sipho or Levina where you can keep
her?' Emily Hope suggested.

But news of James's accident had already
spread and before they could set off Lindiwe
had arrived at reception breathless and anxious.
'James, are you OK?' she gasped, gazing at his
arm and the monkey at the same time.

'I've just sprained my wrist,' James told her,
'but this little monkey has broken hers. We were
just coming over to see your father.'

'My father and Levina are busy seeing to all
the storm damage. The rain got in the research
centre,' Lindiwe explained. 'But you can ask
Paul if you can put her in one of the enclosures.'

There were several enclosures at the centre used mainly when animals had to be caught and brought in for treatment. Paul was Sipho's deputy manager. Lindiwe reached over and stroked the monkey's face. 'And after that you can stay and have some *sudza*.' Mandy and James grinned at one another; they had grown to like the porridge made from ground-up maize meal.

'I think I might be a bit hungry,' James said, taking his glasses from Mrs Hope and putting them on.

'Well, that *proves* James is well on his way to recovery!' laughed Mr Hope, as James flushed red. 'Right, I've offered to give Tony a hand,' he added, 'to see what storm damage there is. He's waiting to go out now.'

'I'd like a shower and a rest,' Emily Hope said. 'I've already had enough excitement for one morning.'

Mandy and James met up with David and Sophie in reception and while Lindiwe went off to her house at the centre to boil up the ground maize meal for the *sudza*, David and Sophie offered to help settle the monkey in.

They found Paul at the centre and he directed them to an empty, wire-covered enclosure. There was a hutch under some shady acacia trees. Mandy held the monkey and watched as David made her a bed with fresh hay. James found a big bowl for water and Sophie ran to ask the chef for some fruit to tempt the monkey when she woke up.

'See, little monkey,' Mandy crooned to her, 'Everyone is helping to make sure you get better.'

Sophie brought back a packet of biscuits as well as the fruit, and she broke two up, putting them beside the hay. When Mandy was sure the monkey had everything she needed she carefully laid her down. Only then would she go to the Ngomanes' house to eat.

Lindiwe had put a big, comfortable chair and a table on the shady veranda especially for James, while Mandy, David and Sophie sat on the steps and tucked into the delicious *sudza*. After breakfast, Mandy insisted James rested while she helped Lindiwe clear up. David and Sophie went to feed the eland and the hornbill. When they had finished washing the dishes,

Lindiwe looked outside and beckoned Mandy to the doorway. James was sound asleep.

'We should let him sleep,' Mandy said. 'Let's go for a walk.' She didn't want to leave James, but she was still feeling a bit too shaken up to sit quietly. She thought that a walk would do her good.

'Look at the pool!' Mandy gasped when they reached the resort.

Branches and leaves covered the surface of the water and part of a broken lounger stuck up in the shallow end.

'Let's clear this up,' Lindiwe said, running to a small hut beside the eating area.

'I'll pull the lounger out,' Mandy called after her, taking off her shoes and wading into the water. She heaved it out and placed it on the grass. Lindiwe came back with two fishing-nets and between them they fished out as many of the branches and leaves from the pool as they could.

'That's saved someone a job,' Lindiwe said, half an hour later, when the pool was clean again.

'Isn't there anything else we could do?' Mandy

asked, as they wandered around the resort and saw everyone working.

'Let's go and ask my father,' Lindiwe said, nodding. 'He might have a job for us.'

At the centre Sipho was talking to David and Sophie McKenzie. 'I am just explaining,' he said, including Mandy and Lindiwe in the conversation, 'that there's nothing you can help me with here, but I'm sending a driver out to check outside the resort. We need to make sure that our trails are still drivable.'

'Oh – we could go with him,' Lindiwe said. 'We want to help.'

'That's what I was thinking. But you'll have to go out in the truck, and stand up in the back.' Sipho told them. 'I need the Jeep myself.'

'I wonder if James'll feel like coming along,' Mandy said. 'I'll go and ask him. I wanted to check on the monkey, anyway.'

'Fine,' Sipho said. 'Make sure you are all back here in, say . . .' he looked at his watch, 'twenty minutes. Marcus will be ready to go by then.'

Mandy and the others walked across to the house, but James was nowhere to be seen.

'Maybe he's gone back to Leela's Lodge,' David suggested.

'I hope he's all right!' Mandy exclaimed guiltily. 'I shouldn't have left him.'

'I'm sure he's fine,' David reassured Mandy as they stood outside the house. 'Let's go and check on the monkey and then you can go and see if James has gone back to your cabin. And you can ask your parents if it's all right for you to come out in the truck.'

'OK,' Mandy nodded, and they strode off to see the monkey.

As they drew close to the enclosure Mandy spotted James, sitting in the shade feeding pieces of biscuit to the monkey.

'James!' Mandy cried anxiously, running across the compound. 'Are you OK?'

He looked up and grinned. 'Yep, we're both fine, and we've made friends. I think she's glad that I rescued her.'

Mandy was relieved. James looked much brighter than he had earlier. The sleep had obviously done him good. The monkey seemed much perkier now too. She seemed to manage well on the ground with only one arm but

Mandy knew she wouldn't be safe in the trees until her arm was healed.

'That's the very last piece for you,' James told the monkey. 'You've had enough. What are we doing this afternoon?' he asked Mandy.

'We're going out with a driver to check the trails,' she began.

'Great,' James responded, then frowned when he saw their faces. 'Me as well, I hope?'

'We weren't sure you'd feel like it,' Mandy said doubtfully.

'Well,' James said, giving them a wonky smile, 'I don't feel up to sitting in the tracker's seat with this,' he indicated his bandaged arm, 'but anything else . . .'

'How about standing in the back of a truck?' Mandy asked. 'Do you think you could manage that?'

'Show me the way!' James said, putting out a hand for David to pull him up.

'I'll go and ask Mum and Dad,' Mandy said, 'and I'll meet you back at the centre.'

Mandy found her dad outside Eland Lodge.

'Hello, love,' Adam Hope said. 'How's the patient?'

'The monkey or James?' Mandy asked with a cheeky grin.

'That sounds as if they're both on the road to recovery,' Mr Hope said.

'They are,' Mandy agreed. 'Dad, Sipho says we can go out in the truck. Is that OK?'

'If James wants to go, that's fine, Mandy,' Mr Hope said seriously. 'But take care of him. I know we can't wrap him in cotton wool, but please,' he said, holding his hands together, '*no more accidents*.'

'We'll try,' Mandy nodded.

'Good.' Her dad gave her one of his lopsided smiles. 'I'll check on the monkey for you later.'

'Thanks, Dad,' Mandy called over her shoulder as she hurtled back to the others.

Once they were in the truck, Mandy and David stood either side of James to make sure he didn't lose his balance if the ride was bumpy. Lindiwe and Sophie stood near the tailgate.

'It's midday now,' Sipho said to Marcus, the driver, as they shut the tailgate. 'Be back by two at the latest. I have another job for you.'

Marcus nodded, then started the engine and they were off.

The rain had settled the dust and the air smelled fresh. Mandy could see that while hardly any trees seemed to have fallen in the storm, a lot of leaves had been blown about and were piled up against rocks. Most of the trails were clear but in one place Marcus had to stop and cut back some branches that were blocking the track. He used a very sharp knife called a panga. While he was chopping, Mandy noticed a thin plume of smoke in the distance.

'Look,' she said, pointing it out to the others. 'What could be burning after that rain?'

Marcus stood up and looked where Mandy pointed. 'We'd better go and see,' he said, giving one last chop and cutting the branches free.

As they got closer, Mandy saw that a knobbly old baobab tree was split and charred all down one side. Smouldering embers lay on the ground.

'It's been struck by lightning,' Marcus told them.

'Will it die now?' James asked, staring at the massive trunk.

'Unlikely,' the driver answered with a grin. 'Take more than lightning to kill a baobab. Those trees can put up with anything.'

'My father knows of a place where they carved out the middle and made a bus stop of a baobab,' Lindiwe told them, as they set off again. 'Thirty people can get inside it, and the tree is still growing!'

'Wow,' James said, raising his eyebrows. 'I'd like to see that.'

'Hang on!' Marcus shouted suddenly, slamming on the brakes and bringing the truck to a shuddering halt. Everyone in the back clutched the sides tightly and Mandy and David both flung protective arms round James.

'Sorry about that!' The driver pointed up ahead. In the distance, blocking their path, was a big hippo standing on the riverbank.

'A female,' Lindiwe said. 'But why isn't she in the wallow?'

The hippo's skin was oozing a thick, glistening, pinky-red liquid that ran down and hung in strings from its body. 'That's what protects it from the sun, isn't it?' James asked Mandy. 'That pinky stuff, I mean.'

Mandy nodded. 'That's what Levina told me.'

David leaned down and spoke to Marcus. 'That hippo shouldn't be out now, should it? It's far too hot.'

The driver shook his head. 'She's standing there for a reason,' he said. 'I'm not going to chance getting any nearer.'

Mandy looked around. Slowly she began to notice landmarks. There was a familiar group of acacia trees, and an avenue of baobab trees.

'James,' she said cautiously. 'Isn't this where we came with Levina?'

'I was just thinking the same thing,' James said, nodding in agreement.

'This is where we saw Harry,' Mandy told the others.

'I reckon the rest of the herd must have moved on,' David guessed. 'But why has this one stayed behind?'

'If she's just had a baby, could she be bonding with it away from the other hippos?' Mandy asked David and Lindiwe. 'That's normal isn't it?'

'But where's the baby?' Sophie asked.

Mandy could see that the hippo was steaming

in the sun. Lindiwe shook her head. 'Her skin will dehydrate if she doesn't get in the water soon.'

'We have to help her!' Mandy said. 'Something must be wrong.'

'You're right, Mandy,' David agreed. 'Let's get back to camp and tell Sipho. Fast!'

Four

'I'm sorry. I'm really snowed under at the moment,' Sipho told them, shrugging his shoulders, when they told him about the hippo. 'The animal was standing by the wallow you say, not apparently injured, so what makes you think something is wrong?' he asked, looking at the row of worried faces.

'Well, it was out in the hot sun,' David replied, 'and it didn't back off or attempt to charge.'

'Sometimes hippos do come out in the afternoons,' Sipho said. 'The young ones like to play then. It's not anything to worry about.'

'Please, Sipho,' Mandy begged. 'Just come and look. I *know* something's wrong.'

'Mandy, I will later, I promise, when I've sorted all these jobs out.' Sipho said wearily.

Mandy swallowed hard. 'But it will be nearly dark then,' she persisted, blinking hard to keep back a tear. '*Please* won't you come now?'

'You're all really convinced,' Sipho said, spreading his hands wide, 'that this hippo is in trouble?'

'Yes!' they said with one voice, nodding vigorously. Mandy hardly dared hope that he would change his mind.

'All right,' Sipho said, sighing deeply. 'I suppose I'll have no peace until I agree. We'll take the Jeep. Lindiwe, go to the house and get my good binoculars for me, please. And Mandy, would you go into the centre and tell Levina I would like her to come as well? The hippo study is her domain.'

Mandy's heart lifted as she ran. Sipho and Levina would find out what was wrong with the hippo and sort it out. Sophie and David walked across to reception to let their parents know what was going on and to ask them to relay the information to the Hopes. The generator was working and the radio was back in service. Everything was almost back to normal.

'Will you come?' Mandy pleaded, having explained to Levina that Sipho wanted her to come out and see a hippo.

'I have to wait for the result of this blood test and then I'll join you,' Levina told Mandy. 'Just a couple of minutes or so.'

Just then, Sipho arrived with the Jeep and they all piled in and waited for Levina.

'Does your arm hurt, James?' Mandy asked her friend.

'Mmm,' James nodded. 'It does a bit. But I don't want it to spoil the rest of my holiday, so I'm not going to think about it. Look, here comes Levina.'

Levina hurried across to the Jeep and got in the front beside Sipho. 'Now, what exactly is *wrong* with this hippo?' she said, turning in her seat to look at them.

'Well,' David began, then faltered and looked at the others.

Mandy took a deep breath and launched into an explanation. 'It was acting strangely,' she said thoughtfully, 'I can't explain what I mean but it wasn't ... well, it didn't seem happy. That's it!' Mandy realised what had been bothering her about the hippo. 'It seemed tense!'

'It seemed tense,' Levina repeated slowly, frowning.

Mandy blushed and hoped Levina wouldn't laugh at her. 'I know it sounds a stupid way to explain it,' she said, 'but I *know* something's wrong.'

'It's not stupid at all, Mandy,' Levina said with a broad smile. 'I think that's a perfect way to explain it. I know just what you mean!'

'If we approach from downriver we might get a better view,' Sipho told David, who nodded in agreement.

Mandy clenched her fists when they reached the avenue of baobab trees. 'I wonder what we'll find?' she said to James, as they exchanged worried looks.

Instead of following the track and driving up to the acacia trees, Sipho left the track and drove across to the river. Then, slowly and carefully, he drove the Jeep between the trees, following the winding stream up towards the hippo wallow.

The hot sun beat down on them and Mandy was glad they were wearing their hats. What would the sun be doing to the hippo, though? Mandy felt the Jeep slow and shudder to a halt. She could hardly bear to look.

'You were right, all of you,' Levina said softly. 'There *is* something wrong.'

Mandy saw that the hippo stood in exactly the same place. It hadn't changed position at all.

Both Levina and Sipho were studying the animal through their binoculars.

'Apart from looking very dry she doesn't seem injured or in trouble,' Levina said in a puzzled voice. 'But, like you, Mandy, I am getting a feeling about this creature. Why doesn't she go in the wallow, when there's water in it?'

Sipho handed his binoculars to David in the back. 'I'll try and get a little closer to her,' he said, starting the engine and edging forward.

'Look! There's a tree on the riverbank,' Mandy observed. 'I didn't notice that when we were here the other night.'

'Perhaps it came down in the storm, Mandy,' Levina, said refocusing her binoculars. 'Ah, yes, that's recent.' She was silent for a few seconds then she took a sharp intake of breath. 'What's that beside it, David, can you see?'

David pointed the glasses in the direction Levina indicated. 'It looks like a baby hippo!' he exclaimed. Mandy felt her heart twist as fear shot through her.

'Let me see David, *please*,' Mandy begged. David handed her the binoculars and, with trembling hands, she tried to focus, dreading what she might see. Holding her breath and trying to keep her hands absolutely still, Mandy looked long and hard through the binoculars. *Please don't let it be a baby hippo!* she pleaded silently. At first she couldn't make anything out, then, all of a sudden, she could clearly see the head of a baby hippo sticking out of the mud on the riverbank, its body buried under the mud. The tip of one of its ears was missing. 'It's Harry!' Mandy closed her eyes and groaned.

'Let me have a look,' Sipho put his hand out for the binoculars. 'This must have happened last night in the storm,' he said as he watched.

'The tree probably fell and trapped him, or he could have fallen down the slippery riverbank and got wedged in the mud.'

'The riverbank is full of holes where creatures live; he could have got stuck in one,' Levina said cautiously. 'That's why the big hippo won't move. It's his mother and she won't leave him.'

'We've got to get him out!' Mandy said urgently. 'He could die out of water, couldn't he?'

Levina turned to face Mandy. 'We have to face the fact that he may have died already, I'm afraid, Mandy,' she told her gently. 'He doesn't seem to be moving at all.'

'Perhaps that's just because he's stuck,' James offered. 'Maybe he's given up struggling.'

'You could be right, James,' Sipho said. 'He's very small. He could just be exhausted.'

'The fact is, if he *is* alive, he needs his mother's milk to survive,' Levina pointed out.

Mandy's mind was racing. Why weren't they doing something? Why were they just sitting here talking? Every part of her wanted to be out of the Jeep and over there pulling Harry free and reuniting him with his mother. She looked at James, his face anxious and full of concern.

'If he *is* alive, he has two things going for him,' Sipho said optimistically. 'His head is covered with mud and the leaves on the fallen tree are giving him some shade.'

Mandy couldn't hold back any longer. 'Can't we do something *now*?' she asked, feeling desperate.

'It won't be an easy job, Mandy,' Levina said carefully. 'The mother won't let us get anywhere near her baby.'

'But we'll be trying to help him!' Mandy protested, her voice full of dismay.

'She won't know that.' Levina shook her head. 'She would kill you rather than let you near her calf. That's the problem when working with wild animals. They're controlled by instincts that are so powerful they can rarely be overcome.'

Mandy knew Levina was right, but she felt frustrated when animals, because of their defensive instincts, wouldn't let you help them.

'You don't mess around with hippos!' David said seriously. 'They often attack when they're upset.'

'He's alive!' Sipho suddenly announced.

Mandy had noticed that the research manager had been watching Harry while they talked. She felt a rush of relief surge through her. 'Then we've got to get him out!' she said urgently. 'Or he really *will* die.'

Five

'We need a plan,' Levina said firmly. 'Hippos can be very dangerous creatures. If the mother chooses to charge she would almost certainly kill one of us.'

'She's capable of biting a man in half with those jaws,' Sipho said. 'And we have another problem. You must never get between a hippo and water.'

'Yes, exactly,' Levina said. 'And we have to do that as well as get between her and her calf.'

'Couldn't we sort of drive her away?' James suggested.

'You'd need a tank to make her move, James,' Sipho replied. 'And even then I think she'd come back at the first chance she had.'

'There is one possibility . . .' Levina said, tapping her chin with a finger. She turned to Sipho. 'What about tranquillising her while we pull him out?'

'I thought you might suggest that,' Sipho said. 'Have you ever done it?'

'No,' Levina shook her head. 'Most animals, but not a hippo.'

'Well, I have and it's a very difficult and dangerous thing to do,' Sipho explained to them all. 'The first danger is that when you dart an animal, you don't always know how it will react. She may panic and fall in the water and drown. We'd never be able to get her out.'

Mandy felt herself flinch at the thought of having to watch the mother drown.

'But by far the worst trouble is with their skin,' Sipho continued. 'Apart from the fact that hippo hide is very thick, under the skin is a wodge of fat that immediately clogs up the dart and stops the anaesthetic getting out into the body.'

'But, please, we've got to do *something*,' Mandy said hurriedly. She couldn't bear the wait while the adults discussed what to do.

'Well, there are special darts called side emission darts that work extremely well with hippos. The anaesthetic comes out of holes in the sides of the darts.' Sipho said. Mandy felt her spirits lift, then fall as Sipho finished, 'But I'm afraid that I'm almost sure we've run out of them back at the research station. I'm waiting for a new batch to come in.'

'We *can* help!' David said in a positive voice. 'I helped Mduduzi do an inventory for Dad and I *know* we have some.'

'That's true, the rangers would have them wouldn't they?' Levina said to Sipho. 'It's worth a try.'

'OK,' Sipho said decisively. 'Hang on to your hats; we'd better get a move on!' Sipho started the engine and, turning the Jeep, accelerated quickly across the savannah, heading back to camp.

Mandy looked at James. His face wore a worried frown. 'James, are you all right?' she asked guiltily. She'd almost forgotten about his arm with all the worry about Harry.

'What?' James said, turning to her. 'Oh that. I'd almost forgotten about my wrist with all this trouble. It's fine. Anyway, it's nothing compared to Harry's predicament.'

Sipho pulled up outside reception in a cloud of dust, and they all jumped out and ran inside.

'What's happening?' Mmatsatsi said, taking a step back and putting up her hands. 'Is this a raid?' she joked.

'Harry, the baby hippo, is stuck in the mud,' Mandy quickly told her.

'Is Tony about?' Sipho asked his wife urgently. 'We need to borrow some veterinary supplies.'

'You're in luck, he happens to be in the stores now.' She lifted the counter flap and indicated for Sipho to come through.

'Lindiwe, go and tell Paul what's happened, please, and get him to put some drums of water on the truck,' Sipho said to his daughter. 'The mother hippo will need to be kept cool.'

'I'll come with you to help,' David offered, following Lindiwe.

'And me,' Sophie said.

'Let's run and tell Mum and Dad,' Mandy

said. 'They'll be worried about Harry too.'

Mandy found her parents at Eland Lodge. 'Harry's trapped in the mud up at the wallow!' she burst out, as she ran up the path.

'Sipho and Levina are going to tranquillise the mother and we'll try and get him out,' James told them. 'But . . .'

'But you have to use special darts,' Mandy cut in.

'Sipho has run out but David says the rangers have got some,' James finished.

'Whoa, hold on a moment,' Adam Hope said calmly from the doorway. 'From what I've heard that's no easy job.' He looked at his wife. 'Do you think they could use some help?'

Emily Hope nodded. 'I'm willing if you are,' she said. 'I'd like to go along for the ride anyway, just to see how they do it.'

'Mandy, run and ask Sipho if there's room for two more,' Mr Hope said, closing the door of the lodge behind him.

'First of all, James, let me have a look at that arm,' Emily Hope said in a firm voice. 'Are you sure you're up to all this?'

James looked shocked. 'I couldn't miss this,

Mrs Hope,' he said in a stunned voice. 'I won't be able to help much, but I really want to be there when you get Harry out.'

'James *can* come, can't he, Mum?' Mandy said, hesitating on the path before setting off for the research centre.

'I don't see why not,' Emily Hope agreed. 'So long as he's careful. Anyway, Dad and I will be there to keep an eye on him. Now off you go, Mandy. Check that there's room for us all. James can sit here and have a rest while we're waiting.'

'Sipho said he'd be grateful for any help,' Mandy called, beckoning for them to hurry.

The Hopes and James made their way over to the research centre where Paul was standing on the back of the truck filling big plastic drums with water from a hose. David was coiling up a length of thick rope, and Lindiwe and Sophie came out of the centre carrying buckets. Sipho was already in the Jeep and Levina was checking the contents of her vet's bag on the bonnet.

'This is a first for me, Adam,' she said, packing the dart gun and the two special darts on top.

'I'm sure you'll do fine,' Adam told her. 'And if there's anything we can do to help, you only have to ask.'

Mandy felt reassured that her parents were coming too. She wasn't surprised by their willingness to help, even though it was supposed to be their holiday.

'We may well need some help,' Sipho said, from the driving seat. 'Once that hippo is down we need to get the baby out as quickly as possible for everyone concerned.' He looked around at them all. Paul and David had shut the tailgate and were coming over. 'Gather round, everyone, please.' Sipho called. 'Now,' he said seriously. 'It's important that we all know what we have to do when the time comes. We have to work as a team, OK?'

Mandy nodded, looking around at the others. Their faces were serious and they were listening intently to what Sipho was saying.

'Paul, it's best if you follow me,' Sipho told him. 'Stay well back until the hippo goes down. Then back the truck over to her and get as close as possible.' Sipho thought for a moment. 'Mandy and David, you will be responsible for pouring water over the hippo to keep her skin wet.'

'But . . .' Mandy began, then caught a look from her mum and stopped. She'd been about to say she wanted to help get Harry out.

Sipho carried on, 'Lindiwe and Sophie, you will keep them supplied with buckets of water.'

The two girls nodded in agreement.

'Paul, Levina and myself will be responsible for freeing Harry, assisted by the Hopes if necessary. Do we all understand what we have to do?' Sipho said. 'We don't want any more accidents!'

Mandy turned and looked at James.

'Poor James,' Emily Hope said, glancing over. 'You *have* been rather accident-prone this holiday, haven't you?'

'I haven't forgotten you, James,' Sipho said. 'I want you up on the truck turning the water taps on and off with your good hand. We don't want to waste water, it's too precious.'

'OK,' James nodded happily, obviously pleased to have a job to do. Mandy grinned at him, glad he'd be able to play a part.

'One more thing,' Sipho said. 'And this

applies to everyone. My word is final. If I say run, you run.' He gave them a smile. 'OK, team, jump in and let's go.'

Mandy felt full of nervous excitement as the little convoy left the compound. 'Just think,' she said to James, 'not long now and Harry will be free. I can hardly bear to think of him stuck in that hole. He must be *so* frightened.'

'It's because you were so insistent about his mum that we're able to try to save him, Mandy,' Sipho called back to her. 'We wouldn't have known he was there otherwise.'

Mandy shivered at the thought. Looking ahead, she saw the avenue of baobab trees that meant they would soon reach the hippos. *Let him still be all right*, she thought over and over. *He's such a little thing.*

The Jeep slowed as they began to creep along beside the river. Levina loaded the dart gun and Mandy watched her, seeing the tension in her face. They rounded a bend and finally, there in front of them, was the mother hippo. As Sipho brought the Jeep to a halt, Mandy glanced back. Paul was bringing the truck alongside them at an angle so that his side window was facing the hippo. He opened a compartment above his head and took out a rifle. Sipho looked across at Paul and nodded. He drove the Jeep forward and Levina took aim. Just when they were so close that Mandy thought the hippo would certainly charge, Levina fired.

The hippo gave a grunt as the dart hit her. There was silence in the Jeep as everyone held their breath and waited. A few more seconds passed and then the mother hippo lurched sideways towards the wallow.

'Oh no, she's going to fall in,' David said. 'Right on top of Harry.'

Mandy felt her heart thud in her chest. With all her being she willed the hippo away from the water. As she watched, the hippo took a step back then went down on her knees and rolled over away from the wallow. Mandy breathed a sigh of relief.

'OK, team,' Sipho said, opening the door and jumping out. 'Let's get going.'

'Good luck,' James said, as Mandy turned to help him get out.

'You too,' Mandy said, her voice full of optimism.

Paul turned the truck and reversed up to the hippo. Sipho went over and checked she was unconscious. Mandy, Lindiwe and Sophie followed him. The hippo looked enormous up close. Mandy could see that her reddish brown skin looked dry even though she was still oozing the pinky fluid.

'Right, keep her wet, but don't get the water in her nose or ears,' Sipho told Mandy.

Levina stepped down the bank to Harry. Mandy found it hard to resist the urge to follow her. Instead, she ran over to the truck where Paul and David were dropping the tailgate and waited to be handed a bucket. Paul helped James up on to the back of the truck then went off to help Sipho and Levina free Harry.

Mandy poured the first bucket of water over the mother hippo and watched as, almost immediately, it was soaked up. The pink liquid that the hippo oozed was oily and had stopped her skin from drying out completely but she was still in desperate need of some moisture. The water mingled with the pink liquid and made the hippo's flanks look shiny in the sun. Mandy stroked the leathery skin, spreading the

water and making sure all of her got wet.

'We're here to help you and Harry,' she whispered in the mother's ear, as she cupped some water in her hand and poured it on the hippo's head. 'And you'll have something to eat soon, too.' Levina, who was concerned that the mother hippo would weaken soon if she didn't go off and graze, had asked Emily Hope and Sophie to go and gather some grass and shrubs.

Mandy looked over to the riverbank. She could see Harry below her, and it was obvious now that the situation was worse than it had appeared from a distance. The baby hippo's whole body was stuck solid in the hard-baked mud. Mandy's dad was helping to try to get a rope around Harry, but it kept slipping over his little head, and all four of his little legs were buried in the mud.

'It's no good,' Sipho said eventually, standing up straight and putting his hands on his hips. 'If we pull it any tighter it could strangle him.'

'I don't think it's the answer, anyway,' Adam Hope commented. 'He's stuck fast. Maybe we'd do better to try to move the tree. It must be holding him down.'

As she watched them working, Mandy poured another bucket of water over the unconscious hippo. She smoothed the animal's tough skin tenderly with her hand. Then she looked up again to see what progress they were making with Harry.

Paul was tying the rope around the tree and fixing the other end to the towbar of the Jeep.

'I'll stand behind Harry,' Sipho called up to Paul. 'Just to make sure that it doesn't drag across him when it moves.'

'I'll signal to Paul once we pull it free,' Adam Hope offered.

Paul got in the Jeep and gunned the engine, driving slowly forward until the rope was taut. Mandy could see her dad and Sipho pushing hard at the tree, but it didn't budge. The wheels of the Jeep began to spin in the dust.

Adam Hope's face was red with exertion. 'It's no good,' he said to Sipho. 'The tree is stuck fast in the mud.'

Levina came up the bank to check on the mother hippo. 'I'm afraid we'll have to give her an antidote,' she told Mandy and David. 'We can't keep her down any longer.'

'But what about Harry?' Mandy pleaded. 'We can't leave him.'

'I can't risk this animal dying too, Mandy,' Levina said firmly. 'All her weight will be pressing on her heart and lungs. We're doing everything we can for Harry but we can't sacrifice his mother's life as well. Lindiwe, would you take over from Mandy for me, please? I have a job for her.'

Levina took Mandy over to the Jeep and opened her vet's bag. She took out a bottle of liquid with a rubber teat on the end.

'Why don't you see if you can get Harry to drink some of this formula?' she suggested. 'It will give him some sustenance until we decide what to do next. Don't force him though, we don't want him to choke.'

Mandy's spirits were low as she walked down the bank to Harry and kneeled down beside him. The mud felt as hard as concrete under her knees.

'At least it's a bit shady here,' she said softly to the baby hippo. 'Don't worry, we're going to help you. Here.' Mandy put the bottle to Harry's big lips. The little hippo jerked his head back and sent the bottle flying out of Mandy's hands. The whites of his eyes were showing. 'At least you've still got some energy left,' Mandy told him, as she retrieved the bottle, wiped the teat and tried again. This time she gave the bottle a little squeeze as she put it to Harry's mouth. A little of the milk squirted into his mouth. Harry looked surprised but swallowed it. Little by little Mandy squirted the milk into his mouth until the bottle was nearly empty.

'Well done, Mandy,' Levina called to her from

the bank above. Mandy looked up and noticed everyone was watching her feed Harry. 'Hurry, we have to give the mother that antidote now,' the Tanzanian vet said gently.

Mandy nodded dismally. She stroked the soft hair on Harry's nose as he drank the last of the milk. He watched her as she stood up. 'Goodbye, Harry,' Mandy said to him as she held back a tear. 'I don't know how yet, but I promise you we'll get you out.'

Six

By the time Mandy had finished giving Harry his bottle, Emily Hope and Sophie had returned laden down with greenery to leave for the mother to eat.

'That was a good idea to collect her some food. She won't go off grazing until something happens to Harry,' Mandy heard Sipho say quietly to Levina. 'I don't think it will be long, one way or another.'

Mandy swallowed hard as she trudged up the bank. She had desperately wanted to save Harry before, but now that she had bonded with him she knew it would be impossible to accept his fate. She watched as her dad untied the rope from the truck. Lindiwe poured the last bucket of water over the mother hippo and then passed it up to James who stacked it in the corner of the truck with the others.

It was getting dark by the time they had all clambered back in the Jeep, and Levina was ready to give the mother the antidote. From a safe distance they watched as the revived hippo lumbered weakly to her feet. She immediately resumed her post of guarding Harry.

'I really thought we were going to free him,' Mandy said in a dejected voice.

'I wish I could have done more,' James said, sounding fed up.

'You all did very well,' Levina said calmly. 'It's a very tricky situation. It's ironic – his mother is Harry's worst enemy at the moment. Without her we could work for much longer.'

'We'll try again tomorrow though,' Mandy said, trying to be positive. 'Won't we?'

'I wouldn't want to sedate her again, Mandy.' Levina said, shaking her head sadly. 'She's a weakened animal. It could jeopardise her life.'

'We'll come out and have a look tomorrow Mandy,' Sipho said reassuringly. 'And assess the situation then.'

Mandy felt miserable. She wished she hadn't overheard Sipho's words earlier, 'one way or another.' Mandy guessed that Sipho thought that something might happen to Harry overnight.

It was a very glum party that drove back to the research centre. They dropped a dejected David and Sophie off at the main building – they were supposed to be helping with the *braai* and were already late. When they reached the centre, Emily Hope, Mandy and James left Mr Hope talking to Levina and Sipho, while they went to check on the monkey.

'Hello, little one,' Mandy said as they entered the enclosure. 'How's your arm?'

The monkey peered out from her bed cautiously. She recognised Mandy and James and came out to see what they had brought her.

'You've had more than enough food for today,' Mandy said.

'Nearly a whole packet of biscuits,' James added. 'And lots of fruit.'

'That's plenty,' Emily Hope agreed. 'We don't
want her getting fat. How's that arm doing?'
They stood for a few moments watching the
monkey as she played with a ball someone had
given her. 'She seems to be using it already!'
Mrs Hope said, sounding pleased.

Mandy checked that the monkey had plenty
of water to drink, then they went out and closed
the gate.

'Sipho and Levina are doing everything they
can,' Adam Hope told Mandy and James, as he
joined them to walk back to the resort.

'I know, Dad.' Mandy couldn't help her voice sounding flat. It was just how she felt.

As they reached the restaurant Tony McKenzie was busily serving the guests already queuing in front of the *braai*. 'How did you get on? You're just in time to join us,' he called, waving a toasting fork. 'I've done something specially for you, Mandy!'

Groups of guests were sitting around eating and drinking, laughing and joking. Mandy didn't like to say that the last thing she felt like was being with lots of people, and as for eating – she thought the food would stick in her throat.

'Thanks, Tony, we'll just go and change out of our dusty clothes,' Mr Hope called over.

'Mum, do I have to?' Mandy asked when they reached Leela's Lodge and Adam Hope had gone to have a shower. 'I'm not a bit hungry.'

'I know how upset you are about Harry, Mandy,' Emily Hope said, putting her hands on Mandy's shoulders and looking down into her face. 'But I don't think it will do you *or* Harry any good to sit here moping all evening. And I'm sure James is hungry.'

Mandy quickly looked at James. 'I don't mind

staying here if Mandy wants to,' he said loyally.

'Well, it would spoil our evening to think of you both being so miserable,' Mrs Hope said, opening the door of Eland Lodge. 'So I think you should put on a brave face and make an effort.'

Mandy nodded. 'OK,' she replied. 'Come on James, you can have the first shower.'

By the time they had changed into clean clothes and were back at the *braai*, Mandy found to her surprise that she was quite hungry. Tony McKenzie had roasted corn on the cob for her on the *braai* and they were juicy and dripping with butter. The Hopes and James had thick steaks with creamy avocado pears, and there was a big bowl of salad on the table.

'I feel like a baby,' James laughed, as Emily Hope cut up his steak for him.

Several of the guests had heard about the hippo rescue operation and stopped at their table to see how it had gone.

'We'll get him out tomorrow,' Mandy found herself answering confidently. By the time she and James got round to eating the sticky pastries that they loved, Mandy had convinced herself, as well as everybody else, that Harry would be freed the next day.

But later, Sipho's words came back to haunt her. She couldn't get them out of her mind. *One way or another*. Mandy had just kissed her parents goodnight when she hesitated. 'Mum, can I ask you a question?' she said reluctantly, not entirely sure that she wanted to hear the answer.

Mrs Hope hovered in the doorway. 'Of course you can. What is it, Mandy?' she asked gently.

'Do you think Harry will survive the night?' Mandy blurted out.

Emily Hope thought for a moment. 'Truthfully,' she said in a careful voice, 'yes, I do. But as time passes his chances *will* get slimmer, Mandy.'

'But tonight? You think he'll be all right for tonight?' Mandy asked again, her hopes rising.

'I do,' her mum said with a nod. 'Especially as he's had some milk. Now, get some sleep, both of you. It will all look better in the morning.' She opened the door and went inside.

'Then whatever it takes, James,' Mandy said, determination filling her voice, 'we've got to get Harry out tomorrow. Tomorrow is his last chance.'

Seven

'What a wonderful day!' Mandy said. She was up and dressed and standing at the window watching a distant herd of wildebeest silhouetted against the clear blue sky. They walked in procession, their bodies shimmering as the first early morning heat haze began to rise from the plains. Mandy had woken up that morning feeling confident that today they would succeed with the hippos. She felt sure that Levina and Sipho would have decided on a plan to free Harry.

'James, why are they called blue wildebeest

when they are obviously grey?' she asked, puzzled.

'I don't know,' James replied yawning. 'They just are, and the black wildebeest are actually brown. Ouch!' he exclaimed. 'I just leaned on the wrong arm. And a white rhino isn't white.'

'How *is* your arm?' Mandy asked.

'Better!' James said, joining her at the window. 'Look.'

Mandy could see that the bruising had come out and James's knuckles were now turning a nice mix of purple, green and black. 'Very impressive,' she said with a grin. 'Let's go and see how the monkey is. We can stop at the kitchens and get some food for her.'

Mandy opened the door and they stepped outside.

'Hello, you two, isn't it a glorious morning?' Mr Hope said, sitting at the picnic table outside Eland Lodge. 'I got up early to watch the dawn; it was pretty spectacular.'

'We thought we'd feed the monkey before breakfast,' Mandy told him. 'Then we'll be ready whenever Sipho and Levina want to go.'

'Are you going to come and see the hippos

again today, Mr Hope?' James asked.

'Just try and keep me away,' Adam Hope answered, giving James a lopsided grin. 'I want to see that little hippo freed as much as anyone.'

'Thanks, Dad,' Mandy said, feeling a new wave of optimism. Whenever her parents got involved, things usually turned out all right in the end.

'Breakfast in about twenty minutes,' Mr Hope called after them.

'OK, see you there,' Mandy replied, waving.

They crossed the resort to the main building. The game rangers were up, milling about and getting the jeeps ready for the day's safaris. But most of the other guests were still in their cabins. Mandy tapped on the open kitchen door and waited.

'Come in, come in,' a voice called from inside.

Mandy and James stepped into the kitchen. People were busily chopping fruit and preparing pots for tea and coffee. The smell of toasting bread filled the air. A big man holding a huge knife with a very sharp-looking blade stood in front of them. 'What can I do for you today?' he said with a big grin that showed lots of gold teeth.

'We wondered if you might have any leftover fruit for an injured monkey,' Mandy asked politely. 'She's got a broken arm.'

'I think I have the very thing for you,' he answered, beckoning Mandy and James to follow him. 'Come with me.'

He led them to the other side of the kitchen where there were big baskets of mangoes, pineapples, apples and other fruit. Deftly, and with a speed that made Mandy's eyes spin, he cut the ends from six mangoes, skinned a pineapple and peeled and quartered two apples. 'There!' he said, pushing all the peeled bits and two quarters of apple into a polystyrene box with the blade of the knife. 'Will that do for your monkey?'

'Wow! Yes. Thank you,' Mandy said, her eyes wide. 'She'll love all this.'

'Any time,' the man said. 'But you tell that monkey that when she's better and back up in the trees, she'd better not come and steal from *my* kitchen.' He held up the knife and smiled at them. 'Or else!'

'We'll tell her,' James said, laughing.

Mandy and James hurried over to the

research centre and let themselves into the monkey's enclosure. As soon as she heard the noise of the gate, the little monkey came out of her hutch to see them. She bounded up to James and tried to put her hand in the pocket of his shorts.

'I haven't got any biscuits in my pocket,' James told her. 'But look what Mandy's brought you.'

Mandy put the box of fruit on the ground and the monkey grabbed a handful and ate it eagerly.

'Look,' James said to Mandy. 'She's using her bad arm. It must be healing well.'

They watched as the monkey carefully picked out all the apple pips and dropped them one by one on the floor. Only when they were all discarded did she nibble the apple.

'That's interesting,' James said. 'She must know that you shouldn't eat apple pips.'

'Pip! That's it, James,' Mandy said. 'I've been trying to think of a name for her while we were looking after her. Let's call her Pip.'

'It suits her,' James said, nodding.

Mandy went to clean out the vervet monkey's

hutch while James sat beneath an acacia tree and fed Pip the chopped fruit.

'By the time her wrist is better, Pip will be almost tame,' Mandy told James, as they left the monkey playing and walked back over to the main resort for breakfast.

At the restaurant, Sipho was sitting with Adam and Emily Hope, drinking a cup of coffee. 'Good morning, Mandy and James,' he said. 'I was just saying to your parents that we'll go out to monitor the situation with Harry and his mum as soon as you're ready.'

'I'm ready now!' Mandy said eagerly.

'Sit down and eat something first, Mandy,' Emily Hope said firmly. 'You can't work on an empty stomach.'

Mandy sat down, drank a glass of fruit juice and fiddled impatiently with a bread roll while James tucked into two rounds of toast and honey.

'I'll go and fetch the truck,' Sipho said, draining his cup of coffee. 'See you in a few minutes.'

'What did Sipho mean, "monitor the situation"?' Mandy asked, puzzled.

'The mother can't be anaesthetised again unless it's a real emergency,' Emily Hope explained. 'Sipho wants to be sure that she's all right. She may not be eating, we just don't know. He thinks we might be able to pull the tree away using the truck. As he says, we'll have to assess the situation.'

'But we will get Harry out, won't we?' Mandy said, unhappy that the plans weren't more cut and dried.

'We'll all do our best, Mandy,' Mrs Hope said. 'That's all we can promise. Oh, look, here comes Levina.'

'Good,' Mandy said, jumping up as the Jeep approached. She could see Lindiwe sitting in the front seat next to Levina. 'I can't wait to get going. Where are David and Sophie?' she asked, peering round.

'Here we are,' Sophie called, as she and David came running from the animal enclosures. 'We had to feed the animals.'

'*Sawubona*, everybody,' Levina greeted them. 'Sipho is on his way with the truck.'

By the time they had climbed into the Jeep, the truck had arrived. Paul's assistant,

Anton, was driving, with Sipho in the passenger seat. Standing in the back was Mduduzi, Tony McKenzie's chief ranger, holding a rifle.

'You take the lead,' Levina called to Anton.

Mandy crossed her fingers as they set off. *This time we'll do it*, she promised herself as she watched the truck bouncing along in front.

When the hippo wallow came into view, Levina pulled the Jeep up next to the truck. Mandy raised her binoculars and scanned the riverbank. There was Harry . . . she held her breath until she saw him blink, then she looked for his mum.

'She's gone!' she exclaimed. 'Harry's mum's gone. But why? Where? Surely she wouldn't abandon Harry?'

'It would be pretty unusual,' Adam Hope said. 'Wouldn't it, Levina?'

'Very out of character,' Levina agreed. 'Hippo mothers are fiercely protective.'

'Does this mean we can free Harry now?' Mandy asked hopefully.

Levina shook her head. 'We have to be very careful, Mandy,' she said, looking over at Sipho in the truck. 'What do you think?' she asked him.

'I think we should wait for a while to make absolutely sure she's not around,' Sipho replied. 'Then I suggest we reverse the truck as near as possible and attach the rope to it.' He pointed along the bank. Mandy saw the rope they had attached to the tree yesterday was lying not far away. Sipho continued. 'Then we can have another go at moving that tree away from Harry.'

'OK,' Adam Hope agreed. 'Same procedure as yesterday, then. You shout directions to me and I'll relay them to Anton.'

Mandy couldn't bear the suspense of waiting. James tried to make the time pass by telling the others about the monkey and her new name.

'She seems to respond to it already,' James said, turning to look at Mandy. 'Doesn't she?'

Mandy nodded absent-mindedly. She was staring at Harry – he was all she could think about.

At last Anton started the engine and turned the truck round so the back was facing the wallow. Mduduzi dropped the tailgate and

Mandy's dad got out of the Jeep and climbed into the back.

'I'm not as fit as I used to be,' he joked, as Mduduzi put out a hand to pull him up.

Slowly Anton reversed the truck until Mduduzi banged on the roof of the cab, signalling him to stop. Then Mduduzi took up a position by the tailgate and stood sentry-like, rifle at the ready. Mandy felt comforted in the knowledge that only under the direst circumstances would he shoot an animal.

Sipho got out and looked carefully around. All was still and quiet, not even a bird was calling. He walked slowly forward until he reached the rope. Bending down, he picked it up, looking round all the while. Mandy glanced back to see her mum anxiously put her hand to her throat. Levina and Lindiwe were watching Sipho intently. He slowly pulled the rope taut and Adam Hope climbed down and waited for him to bring the rope to the truck. Suddenly it snagged on a rock. Mandy bit her lip and watched as her dad walked down towards the river. Sipho handed the end of the rope to Mr Hope and walked back to free it.

'Hurry up!' Levina hissed under her breath.

Sipho reached the snagged rope and bent to clear it. Suddenly he stopped. Mandy saw his body go rigid. She looked at Levina and her mum. They'd noticed it too.

'Oh no,' Levina gasped. 'She can't be – not for all this time!'

Sipho turned slowly away from the wallow, carefully stood up and shouted out to Adam Hope. 'Run!'

Just then Mandy saw two jets of liquid fly up in the air from the wallow. Then there was a tremendous *whoosh* and Harry's mother burst up out of the water. Mandy looked at her father. He seemed to be rooted to the spot. His mouth had dropped open and there was a look of both surprise and disbelief on his face.

'Run, Adam! Run!' Sipho shouted, already sprinting himself.

In a flash, Adam Hope responded. He dropped the rope, turned and ran. In what seemed like slow motion, Mandy watched her dad and Sipho running, and saw the hippo close behind them, charging up the bank. Even from that distance, Mandy could see that her eyes

glinted with a murderous light. Lindiwe was standing on the front seat, screaming to her father to run. Mandy heard Anton gunning the engine and saw to her horror that the truck had begun to move off.

'He's leaving them behind!' Mandy cried, clutching at the seat in front.

'No, it's OK,' Levina quickly responded.

Mandy felt a wave of relief wash over her as her dad reached the truck and flung himself on to the back. Sipho, who'd had further to run, was right behind him and landed on top of him. With the angry hippo just a few metres away Mduduzi banged on the cab, Anton put his foot down and the truck shot forward at high speed. Levina had already started the Jeep and now she swung it around and followed them. Neither vehicle stopped until they were safely back at camp.

'Adam, are you all right?' Emily Hope called anxiously, as she ran over to the truck where Adam and Sipho were sitting recovering, followed by Mandy, James and Levina. Lindiwe jumped up on to the truck and gave her dad a hug. David and Sophie hurried off into reception to tell their parents what had happened.

'Phew!' Adam Hope said, running his hand across his forehead. 'That was a close shave.'

'Dad, that was so scary,' Mandy said, catching up with her mum. 'I thought Harry's mum was going to get you!'

'Wow,' James said, nodding in amazement. 'That was some run, Mr Hope.'

'You're telling me, James,' Mandy's dad said with a grin. 'With a ton and a half of angry hippo chasing me I'm surprised I didn't sprout wings and fly!'

'What you didn't see,' Sipho told them all, 'was that when Anton drove off at such a speed we nearly slid off the back of the truck! Luckily Adam managed to grab Mduduzi's leg and I held on to Adam's shirt.'

'Well, thank goodness you're both all right,' Levina said. 'I think we'll have a little more respect for hippos from now on,' she declared. 'Who would have believed she'd stayed under the water all that time?'

'How long is normal?' James asked.

'Five or ten minutes,' Levina said. 'But in my

research I came across a report that a hippo in a zoo was frightened by a dog and stayed underwater for twenty-nine minutes.'

'What I want to know, Sipho,' Mr Hope asked with a puzzled frown, 'is how did you know she was in there?'

'Ah,' Sipho told them. 'That was lucky. I saw a very slight movement, which drew my attention to her.'

'What sort of movement?' Mandy asked. She hadn't seen anything from the Jeep.

'I saw her nostrils appear,' he said.

'Oh, so the two jets of water were her clearing her nostrils?' James observed.

'Exactly,' Sipho replied. 'I don't know why I didn't suspect she might be in there in the first place.'

'Probably because she stayed under for at least fifteen minutes,' Levina said.

'Right, I think my legs will allow me to get out now,' Adam Hope said, standing up. 'I'm not as unfit as I thought, after all.'

Mandy smiled. She was relieved that her father and Sipho were safe, but there was another worrying thought at the forefront of her mind. *What about Harry?* How were they going to help the baby hippo now?

Eight

'I'm sorry, Mandy,' Sipho said when Mandy brought up the question of Harry. 'I just don't know what to suggest next.'

'I'm reluctant to risk sedating the mother again,' Levina added sadly. 'She's in a weakened condition at the moment. And she must be quite traumatised by the plight of her calf. We don't want to lose them both.'

'But she didn't look weak when she ran out of the wallow, did she?' Mandy said. 'She looked big and strong.'

'And she seemed to have lots of energy,' James added.

'Can't we try again?' Mandy asked. 'Just one more go,' she pleaded. 'For Harry's sake?'

'I don't want to take a chance,' Levina said, shaking her head. 'And don't forget, until new supplies arrive we only have one dart left.'

Sipho looked at his watch and jumped off the truck. 'Mandy, I'm sorry, but I've already lost the morning to the hippos. Levina and I have to get on with our other work now. If any of you have any further ideas I will assist you as much as possible. But I'm afraid that's all I can offer.' He turned and walked off to the research centre with Levina.

Adam Hope climbed down and put his arm round Mandy's shoulders. 'I know it's difficult, love, but, as you've learned, life isn't always easy for wild animals,' he said gently. 'Sometimes there's just nothing that can be done to help and you have to let nature take its course.'

'But, Dad, we could try just once more,' Mandy said with a catch in her voice. 'We can't just leave Harry to die! It's not fair. He's depending on us and we're letting him down.'

Adam Hope sighed. 'Mandy, it's not that any of us are *unwilling* to help,' he said. 'Sipho and Levina desperately want to save the little hippo. It's just that we don't see how we can do it without terrible risk to the mother. And if she dies, then where will we be?'

'I know, Dad,' Mandy said, holding back the tears that were stinging her eyes. 'But I just can't stop thinking about Harry.'

'You have to let him go, Mandy. There's nothing more we can do,' Emily Hope said. 'We must be guided by Levina and Sipho. After all, they are in charge here.'

'My father would do something if he could,' Lindiwe said seriously. 'But we can't save *all* the animals. *Some* have to die.'

'It doesn't seem fair that one of them has to be Harry!' James put in, waving at David and Sophie who were crossing the compound to join them.

'That's the trouble, James,' Adam Hope said solemnly. 'Nature isn't fair and there's nothing we can do about that.'

Mandy swallowed hard and wiped away a tear. 'OK,' she said. 'I'll try not to think about him.'

'Now,' Emily Hope said, 'How about some lunch?'

One by one they all shook their heads. 'No one's hungry, Mum,' Mandy said.

'Let's go and check on Pip then,' David said. 'I don't feel like doing much else now.'

'Nor do I,' Lindiwe said, shrugging her shoulders.

'We'll see you later,' Mandy said to her parents, trying to sound brave.

As they walked across the compound Mandy turned around and saw her mum and dad's worried faces still watching her. She waved and gave them a smile. She knew they didn't like to see her upset.

Pip got very excited when Mandy and James entered her enclosure. David and Sophie couldn't get over how tame she had become.

'She won't want to go back to her troop if we're not careful,' Lindiwe pointed out.

'Doesn't matter,' David said. 'She can be like Dassie and do what she likes. Dad won't mind.'

Mandy dropped wearily to the ground and leaned back against an acacia tree.

'You OK?' James asked, sitting down beside her.

Mandy screwed up her nose. 'Not really, I just feel so . . . so . . . useless. I promised Harry we'd get him out and now I've let him down.'

'It's not your fault,' James said. 'You did everything you could. It's no one's fault.'

Pip came over and tried their pockets for biscuits.

'I'll go and get her some,' Sophie offered, as David and Lindiwe sat on the ground opposite Mandy.

'You'll spoil her,' Mandy said, managing a grin as Pip curled up on her lap. 'I wish Harry had been as lucky as you,' she said, stroking the monkey's soft fur. Suddenly the monkey became alert. She leaned over and her quick little hands began digging in the dust.

'What are you digging for?' Mandy said, bending sideways to see. 'Oh, a grasshopper. She's using her bad hand more and more,' she observed, as the monkey popped the insect into her mouth. 'That's good, digging will strengthen it . . .' Mandy suddenly had a thought.

'Mandy? What's wrong?' Lindiwe asked, her voice worried. Mandy was biting her lip and staring into the distance. 'Mandy?' Lindiwe repeated. 'Talk to me.'

'Nothing's wrong!' Mandy said firmly. 'In fact everything might be all right. Pip has just given me a brilliant idea.'

Everybody waited as Mandy put the monkey on the ground and stood up, hands on hips. 'I don't know why I didn't think of it before,' she said. 'Why don't we *dig* Harry out?'

'It's a good idea, Mandy, but what about the

mother hippo?' David asked. 'She won't stand around and watch. We know that from this morning.'

Mandy thought for a minute. 'Right. Well, she'll have to be sedated. If Sophie and James can keep the mother cool with water, David, you, Lindiwe and I can do the digging.' Mandy thought for a moment. 'I bet Mum and Dad will help too. Then the mother hippo would only need to be sedated for a little while.' Mandy felt her spirits begin to rise. Her plan *had* to work.

'So we just need to persuade Levina,' James said.

'Let's start by organising the whole rescue properly,' Mandy said. 'First we need shovels and forks.'

'We've got loads in the stores,' David said enthusiastically. 'I'll ask Dad if we can borrow some. Come on, you can help me,' he said to Sophie, who'd just arrived back with a little packet of biscuits.

'Help you do what?' Sophie asked in a bewildered voice, as she handed the biscuits to Mandy.

'I'll fill you in on the way,' David told her.

'We'll need a bottle of formula for Harry,' Mandy said, looking at Lindiwe.

'No problem – I can get that,' Lindiwe said.

'Then that's it!' Mandy exclaimed. 'That's all we need.'

'Not quite, Mandy,' James reminded her. 'We still need Levina to agree to dart the mother again.'

'We'll just have to convince her it's really worth one more try,' Mandy said confidently. 'This time it *will* work. Come on, let's go and ask Mum and Dad.'

'I should have known, Mandy Hope,' her dad said, when Mandy had put her plan to him. 'I really should have known. There was I expecting you to forget all about it. I suppose I knew deep down that you wouldn't. So what part do Mum and I play in this?'

Mandy took a deep breath. 'We need you to help us convince Levina to dart the mother hippo just once more,' she told him.

'And come with us to help dig Harry out,' James added.

Adam Hope looked at his wife. She raised her eyebrows and shrugged. 'Trust Mandy to come up with a plan,' she said, her green eyes sparkling. 'Though I *would* like to save the little hippo if we can.'

'Thanks, Mum, Dad,' Mandy said happily. 'Can we go and ask her now?'

'Why not?' Mr Hope said. 'It's as good a time as any.'

The Hopes and James marched off to the research centre. On the way they met up with David and Sophie carrying an assortment of shovels and forks.

'Why do I feel suspiciously like I am about to be put on the spot?' Levina said, coming out of the office and staring at the group that stood outside. 'Are you off gardening?' she said, smiling at David and Sophie. 'Will somebody tell me what's going on? And why is Lindiwe coming out of her house with a bottle of formula?'

Just then Sipho came to the open window to listen. Adam Hope nodded his head at Mandy. She stepped forward. 'I've got a plan to free Harry.'

'Oh, Mandy . . .' Levina sighed.

'No, really, it's a good one. If you will just sedate the mother hippo for a short time we can *dig* Harry out,' she declared. 'Please, Levina, will you help us, just once more?' Mandy looked hard at the vet.

Levina's dark eyes met her gaze. 'Look, Mandy,' she said in a resigned voice, 'I would dearly love to free Harry and I suppose I *could* allow the mother to be put out for a short while, but it's impossible for me to help you. I have already got far behind with my work because of Harry. I have two operations to do this afternoon and I have to go and look at a sick horse tomorrow.'

Mandy was shocked. 'Oh, I hadn't thought you might not be able to come.' She looked up at her dad.

'Is there any reason why Emily or I couldn't do it?' he asked Levina. 'We've both used dart guns before.'

'None at all, Adam.' Levina smiled. 'Either of you could.'

'I can lend you the truck and Anton,' Sipho told them. 'But you'll need an armed guard.

I'm sure Tony will let one of the rangers, Mduduzi or Bongani, go with you.'

'Then that's settled,' Mandy's dad said, looking round at them all. 'We're all set.'

'Oh, thank you, Sipho,' Mandy cried. 'And thank you too, Levina, I just *know* we're going to get him out this time.'

'We hope that you do, Mandy,' Sipho said. 'No one could have campaigned harder.'

David put the forks and shovels in the truck and helped Anton load up some drums of water while Sophie and Lindiwe went off to fetch the buckets. Adam Hope was sent to talk to Tony about borrowing a ranger and he returned just a few minutes later with Mduduzi carrying his rifle. Emily Hope went inside with Levina to load up a vet's bag with everything they would need.

While everyone was getting organised, Mandy walked across to Leela's Lodge with James to fetch his camera.

'If I can't help much at least I can photograph what happens,' he told Mandy on their way back.

Mandy grinned at him. Now that the plan

was under way she could hardly believe it. *This time it's going to work*, she said to herself. *This time for sure.*

Nine

'Everybody in?' Adam Hope called out, as he climbed into the back of the truck.

'Yep.' James did a quick head count. 'We're all here.'

Emily Hope sat in the cab with Anton. She was all geared up to dart the mother hippo. She had the antidote in her bag and because the rangers who had been out with a walking party had returned with their supply of darts, she was equipped with a spare should she need it.

Mandy could hardly suppress her excitement.

This was Harry's last chance. It *had* to be a success. She wouldn't let herself think that anything could go wrong. Word had gone around camp that one last attempt was being made to free the baby hippo and, as they drove past the main building, guests and staff came out from the restaurant to wave and wish them luck.

Anton drove quickly and soon Mandy saw the familiar baobab trees in the distance. When they reached the plain before the acacia trees, he stopped the truck and Mandy could just make out the mother hippo under the trees. 'Stay still,' she begged under her breath. 'Don't go in the wallow.'

'She's weak,' Adam Hope said, his voice serious. 'See how her head is drooping and her legs look wobbly? That run this morning may have sapped her strength. We'll have to work very quickly, everybody. Now, nobody get out of the truck until I say so.'

Anton drove as near as was possible without disturbing the hippo.

'Is this close enough, Mrs Hope?' he asked.

'Yes,' Emily Hope said confidently. 'I can

easily dart her from here.'

'That's good,' Adam Hope said. 'She doesn't seem to have noticed us. And she's certainly a lot calmer than the last time I saw her.'

Mandy watched as her mum lined up the big dart gun and took aim at the hippo. She held her breath. A second later, Emily Hope fired. A perfect hit on the hippo's flank. The hippo looked surprised, stood still for a full minute, looking round, and then sank to her knees and rolled over on to her side.

Mduduzi dropped the tailgate and Adam Hope jumped out. He strode over to the hippo to check she was unconscious, then summoned them over. 'Lindiwe and Sophie, get the water on her as soon as possible, please,' he said, as Mduduzi pushed the water butts to the edge of the truck. 'David, pass me a shovel and let's get going. Mandy, you get down there and start feeding him. He knows you, so you should be able to keep him calm.'

The three of them clambered down the bank to where Harry was wedged.

'Mandy,' Emily Hope called after her. 'When you give him the bottle, make absolutely sure that he is swallowing. We don't want it going into his airway and choking him.'

Mandy pushed the bottle into Harry's mouth and squirted some milk on his tongue. The milk ran out of the side of Harry's mouth. 'His poor little tongue is too dry.' she called up to her mum. 'Shall I keep trying?'

'Yes,' Mrs Hope answered. 'But only a little at a time until his tongue is wet.'

Adam Hope tried digging a shovel into the ground, but the hot sun had baked the mud hard and it merely grazed the surface. 'Get me a fork, please,' he asked David.

'Here, use this one,' Anton said, coming down to help. 'But first, let me cut away some of the branches that are over him. It will make it easier to reach him.'

'Good idea, but we'll need to keep the sun off his head once the shade has gone,' Mr Hope said. 'Can you spare Lindiwe to sponge his head?' he called up to his wife.

Emily Hope nodded and took over Lindiwe's job of keeping the mother hippo wet.

'Try not to spread too much water around,' Mr Hope told Lindiwe, as she scrambled down the bank. 'We don't want to start sliding about in a mudbath.'

Anton went back to the truck and returned with a panga. Mandy knew that these big knives were always kept very sharp. 'Everyone stand back,' he said. Then, with several hard blows, he cut away the branches that had been shading Harry. The little hippo flinched and showed the whites of his eyes, but calmed down when Mandy kneeled down beside him again.

'OK, let's get going,' said Adam Hope.

Mandy could see it was hard, backbreaking work as they slowly chipped away at the mud. Harry seemed undaunted by all the work going on around him and at last began to swallow the milk that she was feeding him.

'No wonder we couldn't move the tree,' Adam Hope pointed out. 'It's buried quite deeply and the earth's baked almost solid.'

Mandy looked up the bank and saw James running from the truck with a bucket of water in his good hand for Sophie to pour over Harry's mother. Mduduzi was holding his rifle in one hand and looking through his binoculars with the other. When he lowered them Mandy could see his face wore a worried expression. He called something in isiZulu to Anton, who immediately stopped digging. He stood up and scanned the horizon. Mandy looked in the same direction. Far, far away, she could see black clouds over the distant mountains and intermittent flashes of lightning which, as she watched, started to come more regularly.

'We'll have to keep an eye on that,' Anton told them, getting back to the digging. 'There's a storm over the mountains and we don't want to be caught in a flash flood.'

'Sipho told us about those – they're really dangerous, aren't they?' Mandy said.

'They *are* very dangerous, Mandy,' Anton said. 'People never believe how quickly a river can rise when it rains far away in the mountains. There have been cases where people have camped on beaches and in the middle of the night, *whoomph*! the water comes down and washes the whole camp away and the people are drowned.'

'But we'll have Harry out before it could reach us, won't we?' Mandy said, standing up and straightening her aching back. Harry had finished the bottle and David had passed her a hand trowel.

'Keep digging, Mandy,' her dad ordered. 'No time to rest yet.'

Mandy crouched down again and carried on digging round Harry's front legs.

'I'm getting worried about the mother, Adam,' Emily Hope called down to her husband. 'Levina told us not to have her under for more than an hour and a half. Can you work a little faster?'

Adam Hope stood up and leaned on his

shovel. The sweat was dripping off his forehead. 'We're going as fast as we can,' he told her.

They were digging frantically now, carving lumps of semi-solid mud away from Harry's body bit by bit. Mandy had just freed one of Harry's legs when she heard a rumbling sound. 'What's that noi—' she began, but was cut short. Without further warning a wall of water half a metre high came churning round the bend in the river. It swirled up around their legs and splashed over Harry's head. Harry struggled desperately and Mandy reached out to hold his head up out of the water. She could hardly keep her balance as the water pulled at her legs. Lindiwe was washed over backwards, but Anton grabbed her and hauled her back up. The fast-flowing muddy water swirled past them and took away everything loose that was in its path.

'Hang on, Mandy!' Adam Hope called out, against the noise of the rushing water.

'I'm all right,' Mandy yelled back. 'But Harry has got water up his nose.'

'The water took the sponge and the bucket right out of my hands,' Lindiwe said, sounding shocked.

After the first rush of water the noise subsided, but the river continued to rise.

'We must hurry,' Anton said urgently. 'This river is rising quickly now.'

Mandy felt a shiver run down her back as the water lapped around her shins; she was already having difficulty keeping Harry's head up and his entire body was almost under the water.

'I can't see where to dig,' Adam Hope said. 'I don't want to spear him with the fork. Mandy, let me have that little trowel.'

Mandy looked down around her, but everything was covered with brown muddy water. 'Dad – it got washed away,' Mandy said, her voice full of dismay at this turn of events. The thought of Harry drowning before they got him out was unbearable.

Adam Hope felt around Harry with his hands then plunged the fork down as deep as he could and pushed against it. It gave suddenly and he fell forward. Twisting his body to avoid falling on Harry, he fell on his side into the water with a splash.

'Dad!' Mandy cried, watching him struggle to get up again.

'I'm all right, Mandy,' Adam Hope said, 'and I've freed Harry's back leg.'

'The river's still rising,' David said, digging frantically under Harry with his hands.

'The force of the water is loosening the mud,' Mr Hope said, as a chunk of mud broke away from the fallen tree.

Mandy was standing below Harry and the water was above her knees. She could feel the force of it powerfully dragging at her legs. She tried to climb up the bank, but as she lifted up one leg, the current almost pulled her off balance and she flung out an arm to grab hold of the tree.

'Mandy and Lindiwe, out of the water, please, before there's an accident,' Adam Hope said in a stern voice. 'You too, David.'

'But I need to hold Harry's head out of the water,' Mandy argued.

'Mandy, now!' her father said.

Mandy knew not to argue with her father when he used that tone of voice. Slipping and sliding in the mud she made her way up the bank. Emily Hope put a hand out to help her up. David and Lindiwe came up behind her.

Wet, bedraggled and covered in mud, Mandy stood with the others on the bank and watched her dad and Anton digging with their bare hands. The river was still rising and Harry was having trouble keeping his head up. As Mandy watched, there was a terrible sucking sound as one end of the tree swung out into the river, knocking Anton off his feet into the middle of the wallow. Scrambling up, Mandy could see that Anton couldn't get a foothold in the mud.

'Now the tree is loose, let me try and pull it away with the truck,' he called out to Adam Hope, when he eventually found his feet. 'The rope is still attached.'

Mandy saw her dad nod. He was holding Harry's head in the crook of his arm and desperately digging underneath him with his free hand. His wet hair was plastered to his head and muddy water ran down his face and dripped off his beard. His shirt was torn and there was a big dollop of mud on his shoulder. Anton was still struggling to get on to the bank. Mandy and David ran to help him up.

Mduduzi stood in the back of the truck. 'I would help but I have to keep watch,' he told

Mandy and David, as they helped Anton drag the rope to the truck. 'It won't be long before we have visitors.' He pointed to the sky. Two vultures circled high overhead.

Anton tied the rope to the towbar and leaped into the cab. The motor roared into life and he pulled forward until the rope was taut. Mandy stood on the riverbank willing the tree to move. Most of Harry's head was under the water now, and Mr Hope was struggling to keep Harry's nostrils clear of the surface. 'Hurry up, Anton,' he called frantically.

Anton edged the truck forward. The rope stretched tight but the tree didn't move. Mandy ran to the driver's side. The engine was screaming as Anton tried to force it forward.

'It's not moving!' she cried. 'Can't you go forward more?'

Anton shook his head. 'This is maximum throttle,' he yelled.

'We're running out of time!' Emily Hope said. 'I have to give the mother hippo the antidote now.'

Mandy stood on the bank. Tears ran down her face and she wiped them with the back of her hand. Harry's head was completely under water now. Mandy turned to her friend. 'We've run out of time, James. They can't get him out. We're going to have to give up!'

Ten

'Wait! It's moving!' James cried, clutching Mandy's arm. 'It *is* Mandy, look!'

Mandy wiped away her tears and looked. Sure enough, centimetre by centimetre, the tree began to move. Soon the water had got underneath it and with a loud creaking sound lifted it free from the mud. Everybody on the bank cheered.

Mandy looked down at Harry. He'd been under water for at least three minutes. How long could a baby like him stay underwater? How big were his lungs?

Just then, Anton leaped out of the cab, ran to the bank and slithered down into the water. He untied the rope from the tree and let it drift away.

'Take his head for me, Anton,' Mr Hope said, struggling with the slippery animal. 'If I can just get my hands underneath him I think we'll be able to get him out.'

'Adam, be careful!' Emily Hope called out.

Mandy held her breath as her dad disappeared under the muddy water.

With the exception of Mduduzi, who couldn't leave his post, and Sophie, who was taking her job of cooling the mother hippo very seriously, they stood in a row along the bank and watched and waited.

Mandy could see the water begin to swirl around Anton. She held her breath. Her dad seemed to have been under an awfully long time. Mandy heard a loud glugging sound like water going down a plughole, and suddenly her dad stood up with Harry limp in his arms. There was an awful, weighted silence . . . and then two jets of water blew out of Harry's nostrils.

'He's alive!' Mandy yelled. 'Dad! You did it!' she shouted, overjoyed. 'You saved Harry.'

'Let's get him up here with his mum, immediately,' Emily Hope said. 'I daren't wait a moment longer. I *must* bring her round now.'

'That's easier said than done,' Adam Hope said. 'He's heavy and the bank is slippery.'

'Tie the rope round your waist Dad,' Mandy told him. 'Then we can pull you up.'

Anton tied the rope round Mr Hope's waist and got behind him and pushed. Mandy, David, Lindiwe and Mrs Hope all pulled on the rope and slowly, with Harry in his arms, Mr Hope reached the top of the bank. He quickly went across and put Harry down beside his mother.

Things began to happen very quickly now. Anton swiftly undid the rope while the others loaded everything back into the truck before scrambling in themselves. Mandy sat on one of the water containers and watched her mother loading the antidote into the gun. She held her breath as Emily Hope took aim and fired. A dart was once again successfully embedded into the mother hippo's flank.

Mandy, who couldn't take her eyes off Harry,

hardly realised the truck was moving. Anton drove them a safe distance away from the hippos and then came to a halt and switched off the engine for them to watch the reunion.

'Why isn't she getting up?' Emily Hope asked her husband after a few minutes of waiting. 'I hope we haven't left her down too long.'

'She is taking rather a long time,' Mr Hope agreed, his shoes squelching as he walked across to the back of the truck for a better view. 'Hang on,' he announced. 'She's beginning to stir.'

The mother hippo lifted her head and looked around. Then, rolling over, she rose to her feet. Mandy's heart was in her mouth as she watched the mother nudge Harry with her nose. He didn't move. She nudged him again and then, very slowly, he rolled over on to his side and opened his eyes.

Mandy saw her parents exchange looks. 'Do you think he's all right?' she asked anxiously. 'Oh, Mum, do you think there's something wrong with his legs? It would be awful if after all that effort he couldn't walk.'

'I think his muscles have just become weak from being trapped, Mandy,' her mum said.

'Give him time. Now, I think we should leave them alone to get on with the business of being hippos. His mother knows how to look after him.'

'And I, for one, would like to get out of these muddy clothes,' Adam Hope said. 'When I volunteered to help, Mandy, I certainly didn't think I'd end up swimming underwater in a muddy river!'

'Lucky you didn't meet up with any crocodiles,' Mduduzi said, grinning.

'Good grief,' Adam Hope said, an expression of horror on his face. 'I didn't give that a thought. I might not have been quite so keen to help if I had!'

'You were brilliant, Dad,' Mandy said, looking at him. His hair was covered in bits of leaf and mud. 'Thanks.'

Anton started the engine up and Mandy turned to have one last look at the hippos. As the truck moved off, the mother hippo raised her head and looked straight at Mandy. 'She's grateful,' she smiled. 'I can feel that she is.'

As they drove through the gates to the

compound, Mandy saw a small crowd of people gathered outside the main building. Everybody had obviously seen the truck returning and had come out to see how they had got on. Anton pulled up outside reception and a tall American man stepped forward. 'Well, young lady,' he asked in a soft drawl. 'Did you do it?'

Mandy looked proudly around at everyone in the truck. 'Yes!' she said, punching the air. 'We did it!'

Everybody clapped and cheered. Mmatsatsi brought out tall glasses of ice cold lemonade and they drank them gratefully.

'Well done you,' Levina said. She and Sipho had heard all the commotion and come over to join them. Mandy told them all about the rescue, particularly the flash flood. 'I'm a bit worried that we didn't see Harry walk, though,' she finished. 'Mum thinks his muscles have got weak from being trapped.'

'We'll go out tonight and see if we can see them, shall we?' Levina said, giving Mandy a broad smile. 'You deserve a truly happy ending after all your persistence.'

'Come on, you two,' Adam Hope called. 'We

should go and have showers. I don't know about you, but I'm beginning to feel like a hippo myself, covered in this baking mud!'

Mandy grinned at him. 'Are they still your favourite animals, Dad?' she asked. 'After this morning?'

'Don't remind me, Mandy,' Mr Hope replied as they walked back to the cabins. 'When I think about turning and seeing that enormous creature coming up the bank, it makes me shiver.'

'I wonder if the mother hippo has got Harry up and walking yet,' Mandy said.

'She certainly got *me* running!' Adam Hope joked, then added more seriously. 'You won't be completely happy until you've seen him again, will you?'

Mandy shook her head. 'Not really,' she said. 'I mean, I'm really glad we got him out but I'd just like to be sure his legs are working properly again.'

'Maybe we'll see him tonight, when we go out with Levina,' James said, looking at his watch. 'Wow, it's nearly dinner-time.'

'Race you to the cabin, James,' Mandy said.

'First one back gets the first shower.'

'Be *careful*, you two,' Emily Hope said. 'Remember, we don't want . . .'

'Any more accidents!' Mandy and James sang together.

That night at dinner, James could use his left hand quite well and didn't need any help cutting up his food. He was just finishing the last *melktert*, a custardy flan, when Levina arrived with Lindiwe.

'I thought we'd go out in the Jeep and check on the wallow first,' Levina said, accepting a cup of coffee from Emily Hope. 'To see if she's moved Harry away.'

Adam Hope topped his cup up with the last drop in the pot. 'That's the way I prefer to see a wallow,' he said, laughing. 'From the safety of a Jeep.'

'You've had an exciting day today, Adam,' Levina said, 'haven't you?'

'More than enough excitement for one day, thank you!' Adam Hope laughed. 'Let's try and have a nice peaceful evening.'

'I don't think I'd ever get fed up with Africa,'

Mandy said, as they walked to the Jeep. She looked dreamily at the big orange sun as it began to sink in the golden sky. 'Even if I lived here for a hundred years.'

'It's not impossible,' James pointed out. 'Living for a hundred more years, I mean,' he said, kicking a stone along the path. 'Some of the tribespeople here claim to be well over a hundred.'

'There is a man who says he is one hundred and twenty-two,' Lindiwe said. 'He lives in a village not far away.'

'Wow,' James said. 'Do you think he really is?'

'I don't know,' Lindiwe said, smiling. 'Why don't you stay in Africa to find out?'

'I'd miss Welford too much, and Gran and Grandad,' Mandy said grinning. 'And helping out at Animal Ark! And James, you'd miss your parents and Blackie.'

'Perhaps we'd better go home, then,' James smiled. 'Anyway, it's school next week.'

David and Sophie were waiting for them beside the Jeep.

'Do you think we'll see Harry tonight, Levina?' Sophie asked. 'Dad said all the guests want to go to see him when they go out on safari tomorrow. It's a good job he's got such a distinctive ear.'

'He's becoming a little celebrity, our Harry,' Emily Hope said.

As soon as it came into sight, Mandy scanned the wallow. She crossed her fingers. The fallen tree had been swept away and the river was almost up to the top of the bank now. Unless they were in the water, there wasn't a hippo in sight. 'They've gone!' she said, as Levina drove right up to the wallow. Mandy felt her spirits soar. 'At least that means he can walk, doesn't it?'

'I would think it does, Mandy,' Levina agreed. 'But you know, sometimes mother hippos carry their babies standing on their backs – to keep the little ones safe from crocodiles.'

'We were lucky no animals came after Harry,' Mandy said.

'You're right,' Levina said, turning the Jeep. 'I was getting worried about the hyenas.'

Levina drove alongside the main river. 'Lots of water,' she said, nodding happily. 'We can go past the dam on our way home. I bet we'll notice a difference.'

In the early evening moonlight, Mandy could see that the river looked deep and fast flowing.

'Wow, that's impressive,' James said, when they crossed the savannah and joined the road. The lake stretched out below them. 'It's *so* much bigger now.'

'This water will last a good long time,' Levina said. 'You may not have been pleased with the flash flood, Adam, but we certainly are.' She drove nearer to the edge of the lake and pulled up.

'I can see the good it's done,' Adam Hope said. 'And the water *did* help to free Harry from the mud.'

'I wish I could see him just once more, then I'd be ready to go home,' Mandy said wistfully. 'Just to be certain he's fully recovered.'

'If we see him we'll take a photo and send it to you,' Lindiwe said generously.

'Thanks,' Mandy said gratefully, but deep down she knew it wouldn't be the same as seeing him in the flesh.

'Just a minute,' Levina sat bolt upright in her

seat. 'Look, everyone, do you see that patch of waterweed?' She pointed at a place about twenty metres away.

'Yes,' Mandy said, following Levina's gaze. 'Oh!' The patch of greenery had begun to move. 'What is it?'

As they watched, there was a great commotion in the water and a big hippo stood up, waterweed hanging from his back. He walked from the lake on to the grass and began grazing.

'It's the big bull hippo that Harry's mother was with the other night.' Levina said excitedly. 'Let's watch.'

'That night seems ages ago, doesn't it?' Mandy said to James.

James nodded vigorously. 'Such a lot has happened since!'

They watched as eleven hippos emerged from the lake and began to wander off in different directions. When the last one had moved almost out of view, Levina started the engine.

'Wait, Levina,' Mandy said, leaning forward and touching her arm. 'Look, there's another one.'

Slowly the last hippo walked out of the lake. Mandy could hardly believe her eyes when, trotting jauntily behind its mum, out came a little hippo.

'Mum? . . . Dad?' Mandy said. 'Isn't that . . . ?' She broke off and a huge grin spread across her face. Mandy didn't need binoculars to see it was Harry. He was running round his mother, nearly tripping her up. His legs certainly seemed to be working well.

'He looks fine after his ordeal, doesn't he?' Adam Hope said. 'Happy now, Mandy?'

Mandy nodded. 'Very,' she said, as Harry and his mother blended into the horizon.

'Ready to go home now?' James asked with a grin.

'Absolutely,' Mandy sighed with contentment. 'That was definitely the most perfect end to a perfect holiday!'

PUP AT THE PALACE
Animal Ark Summer Special

Lucy Daniels

Mandy Hopes loves animals more than anything else. She knows quite a lot about them too: both her parents are vets and Mandy helps out in their surgery, Animal Ark.

Mandy and her family join a village trip to London during the summer holidays. There's lots to see, but on a visit to Buckingham Palace on their first day, Mandy spots a cute labrador puppy, who poses for her camera, then runs off. Sightings of the puppy all over town confuse Mandy – until she reads about a missing *litter* of pups in the paper. Can Mandy help track them all down?